WOMEN

of the

WORKING CLASS

WOMEN

of the

WORKING CLASS

Sue Petty

Front cover pictures:
1. North Wind Picture Archives. 'Smokestacks from steel factories in Sheffield England 1800s.' Hand-coloured woodcut. Alamy.
2. A suffragette is arrested in the street by two police officers in London ,1914. Public Domain, Wikimedia Commons.
3. Detail from Black Panther poster 'Women! Free our sisters'. Public Domain, Library of Congress Prints and Posters Division(yan.1a37759).

For those who came before and forged the way.

Literary magazine publications
"Oxford XIX Miles" in *Copperfield Review Quarterly*, Anthology 2022.
"Tintinnabulation" in *Copperfield Review Quarterly*, Winter 2022.
"Still" in *In Filth It Shall Be Found*, Outcast Press, Oct 2021.

Contents

The Factory Girl

'Here she comes, the Queen o' Sheba.'

Ellen spots the trio leaning against the wall as she walks out the factory gates: Fanny Bryce, big-breasted, one for the lads, a power-loom weaver, like herself; her sulky younger sister, not much older than eleven; the third, she doesn't recognise, but by her jute tunic and dusty mob cap, she also works at the Levant. Straightening her back, Ellen stares into the distance, nose in the air, and braces for the usual verbal onslaught. Fanny Bryce sticks out her foot, times it right, and sends Ellen sprawling.

'Not so high and mighty now, is she? Stuck-up cow.' The sister goes in with a malicious boot, but Fanny sees the handsome overseer coming their way and calls her off. Unmarried, he's a rarity; she's had her eye on him for months. 'Come on, girls, she's not worth it.' She shoots a glob of spit, and they scuttle off down the road, arm in arm.

Ellen knows they are jealous of her poetic gift and comforts herself, knowing she will one day leave them behind to bask in a life of comfort and celebrity. But for now, she gets to her feet—her pride smarting more than her bloody knee—clears her lungs with a rasping cough, and heads home.

Light shines out from the corner shop. Mr Bennie, head down, deep in concentration, is behind the till, a stack of coins and a neat pile of tickets on the counter beside. The bell above the door tinkles, and he smiles in delight at the petite young woman, unruly hair bursting out of her bonnet.

'How are you, canny lass?' He grabs a newspaper from under the counter. 'Here you are, my dear. Delivered this morning. Been holding one back, special.' He shakes his white-haired head as Ellen searches her pocket. 'This one's on me, lassie. The missus loves your wee verses. Keeps her quiet for a while, and that's worth a penny of anybody's money.'

Ellen's thin frame swells with pride, and gripping the coin secured in her pocket, she thanks him.

Dawdling down the street, she thumbs through the newspaper. Page seven, here it is! The sight of her words in print makes her dizzy and fuels her with energy, despite her aching bones. She rests by the front door a moment to catch her breath, then bursts in.

'Ma, it's in!' She dances a highland jig and waves the poem in the air like Saint Andrew's Cross, while quoting verse in a loud, passionate voice.

A smile lights up Ma's ashen face, and she hoists herself up on her sickbed pillows. 'It's lovely, bairn,' she says, wheezing from the effort. 'You get it from your father. He was good with words, an' all.' Ma often reminisces about her 'one true love', Ellen's real father. He deserted them for a better life in America, but she always defends him. 'We were going with him. But you were just a babe in arms and all that time on a ship, I couldna do it. I feel queasy crossing the canal.' Ma sighs, and her eyes grow misty with regret. 'How different our lives would have been, hen.'

'Knowing our luck, we'd have drowned at sea.' Ellen sits on the edge of the bed, holds Ma's shrivelled hand, and in a gentle voice, recites her favourite poem. Lowering her voice, she leans forward. 'Things can change, Ma. Plenty more where that came from. The newspapers pay good money for my verses. We won't have to work ourselves to death anymore. Things can change.' Ma closes her eyes and nestles in the warm glow of her daughter's optimism.

The latch rattles. The way he lumbers in, a little unsteady like he's still lugging sacks of jute around the factory floor, signals he's had a pint to 'wash away the dust.' He'd heard Ellen's 'big gob spoutin' half-way down the street, and his jealous eyes scour the room for evidence of frivolity.

'What's going on?' he rumbles.

Ellen looks down; her eyes trace an ant's haphazard path across the floorboards: stop, start, forward, back, round in circles, like a mad thing searching for something.

'Ellen's had another poem published in Poetry Corner.' Ma claps in excited appreciation but subsides in a spate of coughing.

He screws up the newspaper, like he's wringing Ellen's neck, and missiles it across the room, just missing the ant, now carrying a mouldy breadcrumb back to the nest.

'What've I told you about wasting time on them fekkin' verses?' He comes so close Ellen catches the stink of hard worked sweat and discontent. 'And where's me dinner?' A familiar flash from his alcohol-infused eyes prompts Ellen's retreat into the bedroom. His outbursts are ferocious—hot air and flying fists—but quick to subside. Ma can deal with him. She'll coo and titter, till he collapses at her side and lays his weary head on her bony breast.

Ellen throws herself on the bed and screams into the pillow. She wants to run away, but she has nowhere to go. Last time, she almost caught her death sleeping rough on the banks of the canal. Besides, Ma needs her here. She pulls the Walter Scott novel out from under the mattress, caresses the cover and inhales the musky scent, like a forbidden lover she would die for rather than forsake. Soon lost in another world, she imagines herself the tale's heroine, blighted by much suffering, which she patiently resolves to bear.

M doesn't make it through winter. Ellen packs her bags and slips out early next morning, under a thin moon and starless sky. Owing to countless unscheduled flits they'd done before when he couldn't pay the rent, she is adept at sneaking around in the dark. She wraps her precious books and journals in Ma's old shawl and carefully places them in a large canvas bag. They are all she cares about now. She makes her way down Saltmarket until the intersection at The Cross— four ways. Factory work is all she knows. Plenty of work in Dundee for those looking, a disgruntled hand at the Levant had whispered. A hundred miles away, but she needs a great distance between herself and her stepfather.

Cobbles give way to dirt track on the edge of town, and a vast structure on a hill casts a shadow across her path. Desperate cries emanate from within, or perhaps lack of food and warmth affect her sensibilities and the sound is merely the cold wind searing through spindly branches of leafless trees. A woman stumbles past, a silent bundle clutched to her breast, a mucky child a yard behind, reaching for her hand. Realising their destination, Ellen shudders and strides out, hopeful of her new life.

She sets out early each morning before the general populace hinders her progress, and so she might catch a lift on a cart heading to the next town. She boasts of her poetic successes to the few people she meets and, if in luck, charms a meal with a verse or two. Afterwards, she tells them to seek her out when she is rich and famous, so she may repay their kindness.

At last, Dundee. Dark smoke clouds hang around from the previous day and mingle with the morning fog as it rolls off the river Tay. As the rising sun struggles to alert the masses to the onset of another working day, Ellen gives herself a cat-lick on the banks of the great expanse of water. She pulls a comb through her knotted hair, then heads for the city to find employment in one of the many mills and factories.

She pleads for work. Her experience belies her apparent youthfulness, she promises. But looking a sorry sight, thinner than ever, fit for nothing, she is turned away from place after place. By the time reaches Chapelside, she contemplates ending her misery in a watery grave.

Hiding her trembling hands, she garners her strength to look the power-loom manager in the eye, without breaking down in tears.

James Armstrong hobbles across the factory floor, shouting commands to the workers. 'Big order to meet, lads. Get that jute packed; needs shipping today.' He has worked his way up the ranks from a boy, so he knows how toilsome factory work is, for women especially. With his one good eye, he looks Ellen over from head to toe. He tells her she has arrived at the right time and offers her a job, but warns, 'You've to work hard and regular, lassie, or you'll be out on your ear.' Brushing off her gratitude, he adds, 'Plenty more, the likes of you.' He doubts she's up to it, but his daughter is of similar age, and it breaks his heart to see a young woman in such a desperate state.

Ellen secures lodgings close by—a filthy room in a terraced house, shared with four others. At least she is warm and sheltered from the unpredictable weather. Beggars can't be choosers, as her mam always said. Every evening after work, she wanders over the vast open moors, where the resuscitating sights and sounds of nature replace the deafening machinery and stifling heat of the factory. Stretching her sore limbs, she inhales the heady perfume of spring foliage: mauve heather, yellow gorse, and curly fronds of bright-green fern. A murder of crows caw across the blood-red skyline, returning from scavenging the dirty city streets, and among the thistle's prickly spines, a weeping brook etches away from its source. She ambles past the old pit where the engine thunders water up from its lowest depth and where men toil deep beneath the earth, not seeing daylight for months on end. Then on to the banks of the river, where she sits and marvels at the great dockyard in the distance and watches gigantic liners set sail to foreign places she can only imagine. Like soothing balm to a bleeding heart, her poetic muse comes to her, and words spill from her soul.

She writes late into the night, teasing her thoughts and feelings into verses, poems and songs. She writes as if her life depends on it. Indeed, the doctor has advised her to take a couple months' break from factory work, but rest is impossible with no alternate means of support. Desperate women sell their bodies or turn to the poorhouse, but Ellen would rather starve. Her God-given talent has saved her before; it will again. She signs all her compositions, *The Factory Girl*, and the following morning posts them off to the usual newspapers and magazines.

The following week, Ellen receives a reply from Alexander Campbell, editor of *The Penny Post*. Recognising his handwriting, she tears the letter open immediately.

'Readers want to know more about the mysterious Factory Girl: the talented lass with a way with words,' he writes, and he includes half-a-dozen fan letters in the envelope. Also, a gentleman, the Reverend George Gilfillion, champion of working-class writers, is most impressed with her learning and articulate style. He sends his kind regards and attests: 'The Factory's Girl's wonderful writing is commendable, considering her humble background. She is an excellent example to other poor unfortunates.' In fact, her writing is so popular amongst his readership, Campbell wants to publish a small volume of her poems.

Ellen replies to her fans, in verse. And to quell the readers' curiosity, she composes a brief prose piece about her life, as preface to the little book of poems. She will show them how well she can write. The books she has read, and the suffering she has endured!

'Dear Reader, I have never known true happiness,' she begins.

Yet, despite her misfortunes, all her hopes and dreams are coming true. She clasps her hands and looks heavenwards, tears streaming down her face. 'See, things can change, Ma. Things can change.' She only wishes Ma was there to share her joy.

Two years later

Head bent over till, a small stack of coins and a neat pile of tickets on the counter besides, Mr Bennie closes shop for the evening. He pushes his reading glasses further up his nose and sighs; he is too soft, letting folk have food on tick. The poor are struggling; he will never be repaid.

The door behind him creaks open, and Mrs Bennie's silver head peeps through from the living room. She waves a newspaper.

'Have you seen this, Angus?' Her voice trembles. 'It's about that wee lassie we were so fond of.'

Mr Bennie looks around in alarm; his wife rarely comes into the shop. He takes the newspaper and reads the article:

DONATIONS ARE KINDLY SOLICITED FOR THE FACTORY GIRL, WHO IS SADLY BESET WITH HARD TIMES. SHE IS ILL AND IN DISTRESSED CONDITION.

The Poetry Corner feature ended when the *Penny Post* changed editors, a year ago. Bennie scratches his scalp, thinking hard.

'Jock McTavish saw the wee lassie in Dundee a while back. In a desperate state, he said. In the family way and the father nowhere in sight.'

'Och, what a shame, Angus.' Mrs Bennie shakes her head. 'A canny wee lass and such a way with words.' She closes the door and searches for the treasured little book of poems.

The Nonconformist

Hard leather binding, compressed pages tipped with gold and a smell like Christmas morning—Anne removes the new edition, heart racing. Hearing harsh footsteps down the corridor; she tucks the book under her shawl and polishes the glass cabinet with her handkerchief.

'There you are!' Mrs Godson's greying head pokes through the doorway. 'What on earth are you doing in my husband's study?' Anne fumbles for an explanation, but the woman has more important things on her mind. 'I want the children in bed by six o'clock. We are hosting a dinner party this evening. You are required to help with refreshments and greeting the guests.' She issues instructions with a certain gravitas, befitting a Baptist Minister's wife.

'Yes, Madam.' Anne nods and slips away, gripping the book against her heart.

The dinner party is a low-key affair, despite Mrs Godson's self-important announcement, with a budget stretching to three bottles of Veuve Monier and a choice of triangular sandwiches: tongue or egg and cress. Reverend Godson holds these informal gatherings once a month for a catch-up, his duty to engage with his flock. Anne looks forward to them immensely, not having the chance to meet people outside of work, and an intriguing array of characters attend. Her favourites include Mr James Milligan: once a weaver, now a newspaper editor who also writes beautiful poetry; and Reverend Tweddle, son of a house painter, whose vivid and perceptive sermons illustrate much skill and thought. Both are fine working-class men who have risen the ranks to attain respectability and status. Her employer is of a similar breed: a farmer's son and a self-educated scholar, whose knowledge of scripture is second to none.

Proceedings underway, Anne circulates amongst the guests, proffering eatables and chatting about the awful weather. After a while, she prods a gentleman's intellect on more serious matters. At first, he is reluctant to converse with a mere woman, but once she whets his mind and loosens his tongue, he is more than happy to oblige and finds it quite delightful. As the debate intensifies, Anne, not intimidated by the learned men in whose company she finds herself, argues her thoughts well.

'Remarkable young woman. Well-informed and not shy to voice her opinions,' Mr Milligan tells his host. 'A rare diamond you have there, Godson.'

Anne overhears and fans her hot face with a serviette while Godson turns ashen as a newly hewn headstone and steers the conversation to matters regarding his parish.

At the end of the evening, Anne retrieves the guests' overcoats and hats from the parlour; her duties complete for the day, she retires to her room in the attic. A table and a second-hand bed comprise the furnishings. Rashes of minute holes in the woodwork indicate she is not the only occupant, and though always keen to exercise her intellect, she dares not surmise with what creatures she shares the lumpy, hair-filled mattress. A walnut desk, she insisted on having, lurks in the corner, awaiting her usual late-night scribbling, but too exhilarated to concentrate, she kneels facing the crucifix on the wall and thanks God for her small blessings. She gets into bed, tucks the coarse woollen blanket under her chin and lies awake, mulling over the recent lively conversation with intelligent and enquiring minds. These days, she rarely gets chance to discuss the likes of Ralph Waldo Emerson or Thomas Carlyle, two of her favourite authors.

The evening reminds her of her dear father, back home in the tiny village of Cropredy: of sitting in his workshop as a child, watching him craft shoes while arguing with Joseph, his assistant, about matters of theology and doctrine. She accompanied her father all over Oxfordshire to hear the evangelical orators and itinerant preachers, and, although not understanding, their sincerity and soft eloquence won her heart and moved her till she was bursting with questions.

'You will figure it out for yourself when you are old enough, child,' her father said. A devout Calvinist, he believed religion and faith in God should not be forced, as in the Christian faith. 'You will choose which path to follow.'

When she turned twenty-one, he encouraged her to accept the position of Governess with the Godson family. 'Godson is a good man', he said. 'He can teach you more than any school.' But Anne knew her father had ulterior motives: mechanisation and the mass production of shoes in the new factories were affecting orders, and profits were down in his shoe-making business. He couldn't afford to keep her at home, along with five other younger children. Since she was reluctant to marry without love, Anne had little choice: she needed to earn a living. So, with fifty-shillings parting gift, she left her home and travelled far up North to Carlisle, where Godson had gained promotion. His mission: to bring God's word to the legions of poor working in the mills and factories.

The following morning, when Anne arrives in the main house, Mrs Godson is buttoning her youngest's coat. Frayed cuffs of grey shirt show half-an-inch below elbow-patched sleeves.

'Do keep still, Michael,' Mrs Godson snaps. Her other child, a six-year-old girl, skips around in circles, humming hymns. 'Be quiet, Lotte!'

She snaps again. Mrs Godson is not sleeping well, and her lined forehead and grey complexion make her look much older than her thirty-five years. She misses her family and friends. The climate and the landscape are so different here from her home down South, and the dialect so difficult to fathom the locals may as well speak a foreign language.

Anne sits at the kitchen table and reads the newspaper, awaiting instructions for the day. Godson comes in and plants a kiss on his wife's cheek.

'Would you like your overcoat, dear? It is rather chilly out.' Mrs Godson fastens his collar and hands him a cup of tea. Her existence revolves around fulfilling his every desire; she has no apparent interests and never leaves the house on her own.

Anne wonders she doesn't resent it and buries her head deep in the newspaper, resolving never to marry: a husband would clearly hamper her intellectual development and destroy any hope of her literary pursuits.

Godson spots Anne immersed in the newspaper and sniffs as if infected with a virus. Mrs Godson clears her throat and, catching Anne's attention, nods towards a heap of clothes on the table. Then they depart, taking the children with them.

Left alone, Anne mends holes, lengthens hems and replaces buttons. Settling into a rhythm, she composes verses in her mind and looks around for her notebook. Unfortunately, it's upstairs. She groans, wishing she could spend the morning crafting her poem. But at least her education at the Dame school and those long needlework classes she hated—paid for with her father's hard-earned money—haven't been wasted. A sharp prick on the end of her finger erupts into a bright-red globule and streams down her hand like volcanic lava. She dabs away the blood with her tongue and flexes her fingers until they feel as if they once more belong to her. Bored, she heads to the study for a new read and is disappointed to find the cabinet locked. She sighs and lays her palm against the glass: a transparent but impenetrable barrier to the knowledge within. And Godson has the key.

That evening, Godson summons Anne to his study. Anticipating he has missed the book; she rehearses an explanation:

She wanted to ask, but he was out, visiting his flock. Sure he wouldn't mind and would encourage her reading, as her father had. She took care of the book. No harm done.

But it isn't that. He is writing. preparing his Sunday sermon. He peers over half-moon reading glasses, and the soft evening light renders his balding scalp with a warm amber hue, not unlike saintly portraits in the Bible. He informs Anne her services are no longer required and gives her a week's notice: time enough to find a more suitable position. He is adamant, despite her protests, and with a nonchalant flick signals her departure.

She has never fit in. Even as a child, her mother found her love of books disagreeable— 'A species of idleness' she called it, and chastised her for disappearing so she could read by herself, instead of playing with other children. Folk thought her odd because she wanted to know the reason for everything. She was an outcast at school. The teachers commended her superior knowledge of scripture until they discovered her parents did not worship at the Anglican Church; then the name-calling started: 'Dissenter … Meetinger … Heretic.'

The Godsons are no different. She thought Reverend Godson might understand, being intelligent and educated, like herself. She does her best to accommodate their demands, but they undermine and give her the basest of chores far beneath her intellect. They employ her to educate their two children, yet she runs errands, waits on an endless stream of visitors and does an infinite amount of needlework. What is more, they haven't paid her for three weeks. She has tolerated their ill-treatment because where else could she access the latest publications and meet such learned gentlemen? It is indeed a privilege.

She has most of her father's money remaining, enough to tide her over until she finds another position; so, unable to stay under Godson's roof a moment longer, where she is not wanted, she packs her bags and leaves at daybreak.

Having noticed a property for rent in the newspaper which may suit her purpose, Anne heads to town. On the outskirts, the stench of poor sanitation makes her eyes water, and she pegs her nostrils with her thumb and forefinger; then, recalling the cholera outbreak of the previous year, she holds her breath and covers her nose and mouth with her handkerchief. Thin children, feral creatures wearing mucky rags, run barefoot amongst tumbledown thatched cottages. Tears of compassion blur her vision, and she rushes ahead towards the more respectable abodes of the tradesmen and landowners.

'Look out, wench!' A wagon loaded with barrels swerves, narrowly missing her.

Gulping fresh air, she moves to the edge of the road, where two conjoined houses painted in white stucco stand beside a paved pathway. A graduated green slate roof bears a tall chimney stack, and on the upper wall, six sash windows with glazing bars glint in the sunlight; the three lower windows, large double-arched, afford the building a church-like appearance. An olive-green signboard propped against the open doorway advertises HOWARD ARMS in gold paint; ale fumes and slurred laughter emanate from within.

'Fancy a flash of lightening, my lovely?' a man's voice shouts.

Anne's face burns, and she increases her stride. In the distance, the red sandstone of Carlisle Castle wall runs the length of a lush grass embankment; the ruins continue down and outwards, delineating the town's limits. She hugs the shadows of the West wall and feels safer.

Half a mile away, in the town centre, the castellated bell tower of the Anglican cathedral rises above it all, and Anne hurries in that direction, believing her destination not far. Built of similar red sandstone as the castle, the cathedral's decorative architecture and intricate masonry— around the roofline, in particular— are notable features for sightseers and scholars. Anne stands for a moment, eyes skywards, contemplating the origin and purpose of an angry gargoyle dribbling from a high cornice. Unfortunately, she halts in the path of a vicar, hurrying for mass. They collide, and a thick volume tumbles from his hands and lands in a puddle. She apologises and picks it up, running her fingertips over exquisite gold lettering on the cover before relinquishing her grip.

'Watch where you are going.' The vicar snatches the book. 'Stupid woman!'

His condescending tone hits like a smack in the face, and in an instant, she takes in his spotless black cassock and jewel-encrusted crucifix. He reminds her of the haughty clergyman who came knocking at her father's door when she was a child, demanding to know if the family were all Baptised. Her father, without deference, told him to 'mind his own goddamn business,' and the vicar retreated red-faced, with him berating in the background: 'They'll not be telling me and mine where and how to pray. The foxhunting, wine-supping, pompous sops.'

Anne attended Anglican services at school as a matter of course but found the rituals so bizarre and the discourse so uninspiring she couldn't keep her eyes open.

'All style and no substance,' her father said.

Two streets down, Anne takes a right turn onto Peter Street and arrives at a single storey whitewashed stone building with a yellow thatched roof, squatting amongst a tangle of nettles and brambles. She fights through the undergrowth and cleans a peephole in a cracked windowpane. Inside, long dusty cobwebs straggle oak rafters, bearing husks of starved spiders. The large rectangular room is empty, apart from three upturned chairs and mouse-shredded newspapers scattered across the floorboards. Around the side, an abandoned square-shaped annexe contains a fireplace and an old narrow-back armchair. She would be cosy enough here: a room of her own, with ample space for books and time for studying, far removed from the ceaseless demands of her recent employers. She has enough money for a deposit and a month's rent in advance. The building requires some care and attention; otherwise, it is perfect for a schoolhouse.

Early days, but Anne barely earns enough money to cover costs. Every night, she retires exhausted and wakes up hungry. At least she is independent and accountable to no one. She grows closer to God and welcomes her suffering. The Saints, like Saint Teresa, suffered, after all.

'This hard work is good for me,' she murmurs. 'It is good that I am afflicted.'

She kneels, focusing on the wooden Cross on the wall, and imagines herself there in place of Christ. She feels His pain. Tears stream down her face, and she thanks God for her trials.

She hasn't eaten for three days, and splitting headaches crack her vision. In a flash of light, God sends his angels to watch over her, and she is comforted.

Writing is as important as prayer. It is prayer. God is an eagle on the wing, a salmon in the lake, a deer in the forest. God is everywhere. She feels His presence.

On the bad days, when the darkness consumes her, she explains as symptomatic of her mystic temperament and is secure in her belief that it shall pass. It shall pass.

Anne's classes begin to fill. A kind and knowledgeable teacher, unlike the strict disciplinarians of the church schools who sting their pupils into learning, she is popular with both pupils and parents, and her reputation spreads. But she works harder than ever with little time for books and study: the intellectual life she longs for still out of reach.

In desperation, she writes to Jane Welsh Carlyle, wife of Thomas Carlyle, the social reformer. Her sorrows spill onto the page about how she longs to write books and publish her poems. But the necessity of earning a living is a constant barrier to her interests and intellectual growth. She ends the letter inquiring whether Mrs Carlyle knows of a well-read lady requiring a literary assistant. A message in a bottle; she doesn't expect a reply.

She does receive a reply, however: a lengthy and empathetic reply.

'There is no such position,' writes Mrs Carlyle. 'Even a married woman with substantial means, like me, finds it difficult breaking into the literary world.'

Although unable to offer any practical help, Mrs Carlyle is sympathetic of Anne's dire situation and encourages her to write again to tell her how she is coping. And knowing she is not alone; Mrs Carlyle's kind words give Anne strength to continue.

A hub of political activity, rising socialists gather in Carlisle town centre to challenge traditional ideas about the social order, intent on improving the living and working conditions of the masses. Anne keeps abreast of social and political issues, reading newspaper articles and new publications when and where she can find them, as well as attending lectures and meetings where many prestigious and radical thinkers speak.

She is charmed by Mr Washington Wilks, a journalist for *The Daily Worker*, with his effortless oratory and how he associates with working men. First, he sups ale with them and listens to their sordid stories of brutal and unsanitary working conditions, large families, and overcrowded homes; then, he removes his jacket, rips off his collar and rolls up his sleeves; his splendid moustache quivers, his cheeks grow ruddy, and he launches into his favourite subject: the expanding trade unions. He instructs them to organise politically, for that is their power.

But Anne is most impressed by Mrs Lydia Becker, whose talk on women's suffrage strikes her with the force of an epiphany. Mrs Becker wears a plain black dress with a little white ruffle collar; a dried red carnation pinned to her breast adds a splash of colour and signals her revolutionary inclinations. Her hair, tightly scraped back, has a severe centre parting, which recedes under a black top hat bearing a single black coque feather, which further adds to her cavalier-like appearance. Brilliant and privileged, Mrs Becker has gained much insight from her background in science—her father owns the chemical works in Manchester. Furthermore, extensive self-directed study into plants and animals has taught her that many inequalities of the human world are social constructs, having no justification in the natural world.

Her square face, pale from much learning, turns towards Anne, and her overly large intelligent eyes, magnified behind circular spectacles, scrutinise her soul and comprehend her suffering. Then, with the fiercest demeanour Anne has ever encountered in a woman, she describes how inequality between the sexes in privilege and power causes the dreadful hardships of women—women of the lower classes, in particular.

In Mrs Becker's words, Anne recognises the story of her own sorrows and thwarted ambitions: that as a working-class woman, despite education and a keen intellect, she will never fulfil her potential or contribute to society in more meaningful ways.

Ground hard under lingering frost, the morning freshness tantalises Anne's skin, making her shiver as if the air contains something tangible. She observes sparrows in the garden scavenging for food; if lucky, they find an occasional shrivelled worm under a stone. Tossing a handful of stale crumbs, she marvels at how the little creatures go on despite adversity, with no expectation of reward. And, thus, she reaches an impasse, resigning herself to a lifetime of hard work and the inevitable inability of ever fulfilling her literary dreams.

Yet she vows to do all she can to help her poor working-class sisters in the best way she can: through her words and writing. Believing education can ease poverty, she starts a literacy class for female factory workers; and she sends letters and articles to newspapers and journals regarding crucial women's issues: employment, voting rights and contraception. However, she signs all her correspondence *AS*, not her actual name, for how could anyone believe a woman had written them? Or, if they did, how could they take her seriously? The world is not ready. She is a work in progress.

OXFORD XIX MILES

A hare darts under the hedgerow as a girl and boy head up the turnpike road. The girl walks in the centre, wooden yoke balanced across thin shoulders, tanned knees showing beneath a dusty-blue gingham cotton pinafore, sun-kissed plaited ponytail swaying in rhythm with her deliberate stride. She looks straight ahead, focused on her mission. The boy skips in and out of long grass edging a vast field, arms outstretched, reaching for cabbage whites, pockets of baggy brown cut-offs bulging with acorns and crab apples.

A wooden sign sticking out of the ground obstructs his path. 'What does it mean, Flora?' He runs blackberry-stained fingers over the etched markings.

'It says Oxford Nineteen Miles,' she replies, with an awkward twist of her head.

'What's Oxford?'

The market town is the furthest Flora has travelled, but she has seen pictures of Oxford in books. 'It's a wonderful place with towers tall as pine trees and libraries wider than fields. People go there to get educated, so they can be teachers and lawyers. And even prime ministers, like Mr Gladstone.' A distant train rumbles over a viaduct, and Flora concentrates on the task at hand. 'Come on, Edwin, we mustn't dawdle. Ma will be waiting.'

They are blessed with another long hot summer, but it means a daily trek to fetch water. Apart from rainwater caught in a large butt as it runs off the cottage guttering, the well is their only water source. Nestling in a clearing off the main road, the well is sheltered by a thatched roof resembling a witch's hat; a two-foot-high stone wall circles it at ground level, preventing folk from falling in. A large wooden board, coated in thick clay leans against the wall, with petals, leaves and twigs, resembling little matchstick animals, people and houses, pressed into the surface.

'It's so pretty. Ma would love it.' The boy runs to pick it up.

'Leave it, Edwin.' Flora sheds the yoke onto the grass and sighs with relief. 'The hamlet folk used to decorate the well and gather to give thanks to a water god, Grandpa told me. Looks like some still do, and they won't like it if we steal their flower board.' She lowers the rope into the deep black hole and listens for the splash. The menfolk talk about installing a pump but have yet to start work.

The children fill two buckets with water and hang one on each yoke end, and once Flora has steadied the load, they head home.

The late summer breeze ripples a sea of golden wheat, and a melodious buzz and churr trills from way up high. Purple-pink foxgloves perfume the morning air, and a young queen hums between blue cornflowers and yellow marigolds. Thirty cottages dot around a distant hillside; home to the farm labourers, a rutted dirt track and a labyrinth of footpaths, winding through fields and woodland, connects them. Several cottages stand out with white-washed exteriors and yellow thatched roofs, but most recent additions blend into the landscape with grey stone walls and slate roofs. The children live in 'End House', an extended white cottage, lying at the furthermost point of the hamlet. Their father, a stonemason by trade, earns more money than the farmworkers, so their home is bigger with three bedrooms and a kitchen. Flora, age fourteen, is the eldest of five children. Edwin is seven. There were six of them, but the youngest didn't survive last winter.

Heavy heads of corn, almost touching the garden gate, nod in greeting as the two children brush past. They empty the buckets into the large butt, then run round to the back garden. Taking a handful of acorns from his pocket Edwin calls, 'Daisy. Daisy,' and an enormous black-and-white pig trots out of a make-shift sty. The pig nuzzles his outstretched hand, and Flora leans over the fence to pet it's wire-haired head. They love the pig, but they understand that, one day, their father will ceremoniously slaughter it to provide food for the family.

'Pick us some carrots, love.' Ma's head, wrapped in a scarf made of similar gingham material as Flora's pinafore, pokes through the open kitchen window.

Flora uproots half a dozen, shakes off the dirt and takes them to the kitchen, where Ma dangles a limp furry animal mid-air by its two long hind legs. With a sharp downwards tug and slick tear, she separates skin from carcass.

'Rabbit stew, Ma?' Flora places the carrots on the kitchen table, next to a bowl of white potatoes and a pile of curled peelings.

'We all deserve a treat now and then to cheer us up.' Flora's father's favourite: it's him who needs cheering up. Now and then, a moodiness strikes him, and he disappears into the woods to mull it all over. Hours later, he returns and carries on as usual. Ma cracks a bone and drops it into the cooking pot.

'Ma, what will I be when I go to Oxford?' Edwin pulls on the corner of her red-speckled apron.

'My poor little man, there won't be any college for you.' Ma says, laying the lean, pink meat on the table.

There is a famous saying among the hamlet folk: 'Brains are no good to a working man.' Boys leave school at eleven to follow the plough, as their fathers. Edwin could be a stonemason, but pensive and sensitive he is unsuitable for such an occupation.

With a deft stroke of the meat cleaver, Ma chops off a brown furry foot. 'Here, my lad. We all deserve a bit of good luck.'

Edwin has watched her dissect all kinds of creatures and make tasty meals out of the various body parts. She wastes nothing. He strokes the soft, fluffy talisman, five toenails intact, and places it in his pocket.

Unlike Ma, their father does consider his children's education. Because teachers expect their pupils to work in the fields, the quality of teaching at the local school is poor and does not encourage learning. He started home schooling but was called away on a job in another village, so their education abruptly ended. Although Flora continued to study by herself and was often seen around the hamlet carrying a book. Until folks grumbled that she ought to be home helping her man with the chores rather than wasting time reading. Since her Ma agreed, Flora started to hide her books and read in secret.

Her favourite place is under the apple trees in Grandad's garden. His cottage is the older type with a yellow thatched roof, white-washed walls, and little diamond-shaped windows. All the furniture is solid and handmade, and, in the distant past, someone must have carved the enormous oak table inside because it is too big to fit through the door. Although Grandma died six years ago, her various handicrafts remain in place: pretty hand-thrown pottery, colourful rugs, and beautiful embroidered cushions. Romantic novelettes she loved to read in the evenings are still piled high on the table.

Nowadays, the enormous garden is a jungle of brambles and overgrown fruit trees. But once, Flora's grandparents cultivated all manner of plants.

'Fifty years of marriage and we never owed anybody ought', Grandad says, propping his walking cane against a tree. He sits on a decaying bench near where Flora reads, takes a clay pipe out of his waistcoat pocket, and strikes a match on a stone. 'Aye, we grew all our own fruit and vegetables.

And we owned a cow, geese, chickens, a pig and a donkey. We could turn the animals out to graze on the common land, you see. And what we didn't need ourselves, we took to market. Little else, but we always had enough food. "The closer to the bone, the sweeter the meat," your gran used to say. Aye, we were happy enough.'

Grandad draws on the smouldering tobacco, and Flora inhales the balmy smoke as it melts into air. 'But then they joined up the fields, put it all under the master's ownership, and he paid us a pittance to farm the land for him.' He scratches his grey whiskers and shakes his balding head. 'After that, the new-fangled machinery put men out of work: men whose families had farmed the land for generations. Now they couldn't feed their kiddies and pay the rent. Some resisted, but it was no good. "You can't halt progress," the Master said. They arrested a gang of rebels and sent them abroad. Many left the land and found jobs in the factories.' He knocks the pipe against the stone and stomps on the glowing embers.

The inspector discovers Flora, and her siblings don't attend school and forces them to attend. Self-taught, Flora can write already, but the school insists she learns a certain way, which she finds difficult. Arithmetic bores her and she hates needlework, which girls are taught every afternoon. When girls leave school, they find employment as housemaids or child nurses, but since she also hates housework, Flora wonders what will become of her. Longing to pick flowers, play hide-and-seek with her brother and forage for berries in the woods, she gazes out of the classroom window.

Flora does enjoy reading lessons, though, thanks to Miss Shepherd, the teacher, who, recently qualified, is informed with new ideas regarding education. Miss Shepherd wears a long crimson skirt, a high-collared white blouse and a tie matching the skirt's colour. A wide black belt hugs her narrow waist, accentuating her slender figure, achieved through conscientious exercise rather than corsetry, which she decries as unnatural and unhealthy. However, Miss Shepherd's most startling feature is not her appearance but what she teaches.

'It is not what people own. But what they are like inside that matters,' she says. 'Poor people are as valuable and as good as rich people.' To illustrate her point, she reads her pupils the beautiful verse of John Clare, once a farm labourer himself.

'Being born poor does not mean you will always be poor. Through effort and hard work, some boys have risen above their humble backgrounds to become distinguished men.' She tells them the story about James Keir Hardy, whose mother was a servant on a farm. Aged ten, he worked down the coalmine, but determined the job would not be his life he learnt to read and write. And now he is a politician, helping form the Labour Party, which comprises and is for working people, like themselves, unlike the Tory Party.

Miss Shepherd's teaching blatantly contradicts the vicar's instruction. Every Sunday at Church, he preaches about how they should be satisfied with their lot because it is God-given and just and afterwards leads them in a solemn rendition of *All Things Bright and Beautiful*:

> *The rich man in his castle*
> *The poor man at his gate*
> *God made them high and lowly*
> *And ordered their estate.*

Although Flora notices Miss Shepherd doesn't mention any girls who have risen above *their* humble station to become distinguished women. But Flora thinks if boys can, why can't girls? Why can't she be something other than a servant or a nursemaid?

'Miss, did you learn to be a teacher at Oxford?' she enquires of the wondrous oracle.

'Women may not study at Oxford,' Miss Shepherd replies. 'But we will, one day.'

Flora believes her. She gazes out of the window, beyond the trees and fields, and imagines pensive women wearing black gowns and mortarboards, walking amidst tall towers and vast libraries, their arms laden with heavy books.

After much pleading, Flora's father agrees to take her and Ma to the market town to visit Aunt Clara and hires a pony and trap, especially. Their previous visit, two years ago, was for just one day. Flora wanted to stay longer to explore the shops on the High Street.

Lying midway between the hamlet and Oxford, the market town is eight miles drive on the dusty turnpike. After an hour's travelling, the turnpike widens. A solitary tractor chugs up a hillside, not a farmworker in sight.

'Nearly there.' Her father clicks the pony onwards.

'Thank goodness.' Ma fidgets and rubs the small of her back.

Countryside gives way to a stony road flanked by a neat row of smart, tiny houses, each with a white picket fence, fronting well-kept gardens. Not recognising them, Flora wonders whether her father took the wrong turn, but around the next bend, the High Street and the shops she remembers come into view. The stony road with the smart, tiny houses wasn't here before: stretching out, expanding the town's limits, it is brand new.

Flora's father and her uncle Henry had an awful row on their previous visit. Political differences. Henry believes the Tories support people who want to get on in life. He plans to upgrade his blacksmith business into a garage; instead of shoeing horses and changing wheels on wagons, it will mend engines and change tyres on cars: a much more lucrative enterprise for this day and age. Flora's father believes the Tories and money are the roots of all evil, and he supports Gladstone because Gladstone represents working men. He almost punched Henry's smug face.

So, their reunion is awkward at first. But after Ma advises best not talk politics this time, they shake hands and head to The Queens Head for a pint before tea.

Flora's ma and Aunt Clara are sisters, although you wouldn't know by looking at them. Ma, red-cheeked and robust, stands hands-on-hips, awaiting the next challenge; whereas, Clara, ghostly pale and thin, wrings her hands, unsure what to do. Unable to bear children, Clara puts her energy into the home: not a new house—an Edwardian terrace with two large bay windows looking out on the street—but they have gas and water on tap and fitted carpets.

Decorated in lime-green patterned wallpaper, the parlour walls are punctuated with portraits of sombre strangers, who Henry likes to think are distinguished relatives. In the corner, a white wrought-iron birdcage decorated with curls and volutes hangs from the ceiling—home to a solitary yellow canary, which stands motionless on a perch.

'Oh, he's happy enough,' Clara says, noticing Flora's disapproving frown. 'Sings his little heart out, every morning. Henry bought him to keep me company.'

Flora pokes the tip of her finger through the narrow bars but withdraws as the bird flutters like a mad thing.

Over the mantlepiece, a vast gilt-framed mirror reflects Ma's shocked expression; unused to seeing herself, she studies a dozen little ornaments instead—what she calls 'useless knick-knacks'—lining the mantle surface. The centrepiece, a cluster of upturned crimson petals, grabs her attention.

'Oh, how beautiful.' She reaches out to touch it.

'A lotus flower. It's not real.' Clara crushes it in her palm, then it springs back into shape. 'Made of silk. Real ones grow in China out of thick mud. The florist sells them in town. We can go tomorrow if you like?'

Excited, Flora claps her hands, then goes to the bathroom and washes them with hot water and lavender-scented soap in the white porcelain sink, for a third time.

Streams of vehicles rattle up and down High Street: horse-drawn carriages, wagons and carts, and chugging motor cars belonging to wealthy business owners. Flora, Ma and Clara wait on the kerbside for a gap. A flurry of bicycles breeze past —another innovation since Flora's last visit. Even women cycle, skirts tucked between legs, ankles flashing.

'Wish we owned a bicycle to fetch water from the well—a bucket on each handlebar,' Ma says, laughing.

'They're evil contraptions, Henry reckons,' Clara says. 'Women gallivanting all over the place with the wind distorting their features. There'll be no pretty women left soon, he says.'

Ma snorts in disbelief, while Flora's eyes trace a trio of cycling ladies zooming into the horizon.

'Quick. Now!' A lull in traffic, and Clara leads them across the busy road.

Safe on the other side, Flora shakes her purse, ensuring her pennies are intact, and Ma squashes her nose against a hat shop window.

'Goodness, so many styles and colours. I could spend the entire day making up my mind.' Accustomed to buying essentials from the small store in the rear of the Public House and anything else from the peddler's bulging suitcase, shops dedicated to retail one product are a real novelty for Ma.

A fancy, broad-brimmed hat with a low crown, adorned with flowers, lace, ribbons and feathers takes her fancy: a real head-turner at Church. Egged-on by Clara, she almost buys it but backs down, guilt-stricken: 'It's foolish. Besides, winter's coming.'

Before leaving town, Ma takes Flora with her to visit an old friend, Adelaide. Jolly and overweight, with greying hair and a wide amiable smile, stemming from natural gregariousness rather than cunning for profit, Adelaide is the town's postmistress. Behind the till, as normal, she leans over the post office counter and hugs them both.

'Quite the young lady,' she says, gasping at how much Flora has grown. 'And so pretty.' Flora blushes and folds her arms over her chest, conscious of her budding breasts. Adelaide turns to Ma. 'What's she going to be when she leaves school? Won't be long now.'

'We don't know, yet.' Ma sighs. 'Always got her head in books these days.'

The doorbell tinkles and Adelaide flashes a smile at a small, elderly woman.

'Good afternoon, Mrs Smith. What can I do for you?'

'I'd like to post this birthday card to my Ethel, please.' Mrs Smith's only daughter works as a maid at the old hall. 'She's sixteen on Friday. Haven't seen her for six months. They won't let her have any time off.'

'At least you know she's in safe hands, Mrs Smith.' Adelaide tears a single purple and blue stamp off a sheet. 'Isn't it wonderful what they can do nowadays?' She holds the stamp at arm's length. 'The first one made in two colours, and all in honour of Her Majesty's Golden Jubilee. God bless her!' She presses the stamp onto the envelope corner and pops it in the mail sack. '5d. Mrs Smith, thank you. Your daughter will appreciate it, I'm sure.' The old woman leaves, and Adelaide resumes her conversation with Ma.

Leaving them to it, Flora inspects a rack of stationery on the wall, containing envelopes, writing paper, calendars, and an assortment of pens. She wants to buy a notebook and some ink if her pennies stretch. Since hearing Miss Shepherd recite John Clare's poems, she has begun composing her own, about nature and the hamlet.

A mechanical clanking sound, coming from the far wall, distracts her, and she sees a young man, with smooth slicked-back hair and a pleasant aroma—the post office clerk— pressing keys up and down on a strange contraption.

'It's a telegraph machine,' he announces, noticing Flora's inquisitive stare. 'It transmits messages in minutes and across miles.' Eager to show off the new installation, he beckons her over. His wife works in the hat shop. They live in one of the smart, tiny houses on the edge of town, known as the Villas. Members of a new emerging class, they work hard and take advantage of the mass-produced, inexpensive commodities on their doorstep. They take pride in their personal appearance and their homes and exercise restraint on limiting the size of their families.

'Yes, it'll revolutionise communication around these parts.' The young man explains how the machine works.

Flora listens hard, trying to understand.

Back home, amongst the wide-open spaces and heavy silence of the hamlet, Flora has difficulties returning to her old routine. The market town, like Miss Shepherd, has awakened something in her. Curiosity? The spirit of adventure? The restlessness of youth? Whatever it is, she can't settle. She buries herself in books and concentrates on her writing.

Ma receives a letter from Adelaide, several weeks later: she's not getting any younger and is thinking of retirement. She wants Flora to come and work for her at the Post Office. She will train her, of course.

Flora could learn a lot from Adelaide, Ma says. Adelaide enjoys what town life offers, but she is a clever woman. Apart from running her own business, she reads the newspapers and knows about current affairs. She keeps her eye on the stock market and even has a few shares secreted away.

We are only a few miles down the turnpike, if you ever need us, her father says.

It is Flora's decision.

Her father hires the pony and trap, once more. Flora packs her books and her few belongings in an old leather trunk; with few material comforts, she has grown-up and taken her pleasure and entertainment in the woods and fields enveloping the hamlet. She sets out early one morning with the mist hanging on the horizon, and though she may seldom return, she takes with her an enduring love and an eternal bond to her childhood home. The old way of life is disappearing; it is sad but exciting too, and she wants to be a part of it.

She Sells Seashells

The remote seaside town is quieter now. Tucked away for the winter, the gentlefolk have returned to their warm homes, inland. Mary walks the seashore scouring the precarious blend of shale and shingle, black cloak billowing, thick woollen bonnet anchored under her chin. A blast of salt wind pushes her off balance. Underweight for her twenty-three years, not weak though; years treading the rugged shoreline and negotiating the steep cliff paths have made her sinewy and strong. Last night's storm loosened the cliff face and gullies of rainwater surge through cracks and crevices, so she is extra careful this morning. She leans forward, then swoops like a scavenging gull to grab a nodule of rock in mud-pitted fingers. She taps it with a small hammer. It sounds promising. Two more sharp taps in the right place and the rock cracks open, revealing an ingrained spiral like a snail's shell: another ammonite, not perfect but worth a few pennies cleaned up. With a satisfied nod, she places it in a wicker basket looped over her arm.

The cliffs stretch ten miles between Lyme Regis and Charmouth. High tide cuts East Cliff off from the mainland: low tide reveals an expanse of wet sand and rock ledges with hundreds of shimmering rock pools. Mary pauses to inspect a hollow in the lower cliff: a scar from an excavation ten years earlier where, aged twelve, she discovered her first monster. The strange skull with large saucer-shaped eyes and a long snout stuck out of the rock. Seventeen feet long, the complete fossil caused great excitement. After much deliberation, the scientists named it Ichthyosaurus, meaning 'fish lizard', and donated it to London Museum. They paid Mary twenty-three pounds for her trouble.

'Tray. Tray!' she calls, and a small black and white dog, tail wagging, appears from behind a glistening rock near the foaming breakers; afraid a landslide had buried him, she sighs with relief. 'What have you found there, boy?' Behind the rock, a cracked wooden crate spills its contents into the receding tide: tea, tobacco, bottles of brandy and some folded material—all wrapped in oilskin. Thrown overboard by smugglers, most likely. Folk struggle to earn a living the best way they can; corn taxes make bread too expensive, even for working men; but the farm labourers have it worse with wage cuts and new machinery stealing their jobs. Revolts are breaking out all over the Dorset countryside: machine wrecking, haystack and barn burning. Mary's father took part in such clandestine activities before moving to Lyme, but her mam stopped him. Just as well because the authorities sentenced six rogue labourers for penal transportation to Australia.

Mary stares out to sea. How far is Australia? Did the monsters live there once and drift across on the current when they died? At least, that's what some scientists told her. It doesn't explain why the monsters lay buried deep in the cliffs, though, and why no one has ever seen one alive. A black speck on the horizon causes her heart to miss a beat. The entire town has kept a fearful eye on the horizon for years: the threat of invasion prompted them to install half-a-dozen cannons on the clifftop.

Despite their worries, her late father would cast a salute to old Napoleon. 'We should thank the Frenchies for our good fortune,' he'd say. He reckoned the war with France made it unsafe to sail abroad: that's why the gentlefolk flock to Lyme for their holidays and why his little fossil shop on Cockmoile Square made him so much money.

Mary squints over the channel, but the ship has gone. She drags the crate further up the beach and drapes it with long twirls of dark green seaweed. She might let slip to Mrs Barrett, their neighbour, about what she'd found. Mrs Barrett could do with a bit of good fortune, too; her eldest, Millie, is wearing a turban, again. Turbans are all the fashion amongst the young gentlewomen, but Millie wears one because she sold her hair to the barber to make fancy wigs and stuff cushions. Mary feels sorry for Millie; her long yellow hair was her best asset.

But Mary's prospects are not so great, either. Her dad died of consumption, leaving her mam with two children, a baby, and piles of bills. The baby died not long after, but she was saddled with the debts. Mary can read and write, having learnt at the Congregationalist Sunday school, but she has little to offer a man. No money, of course; moreover, her unwomanly appearance and brusque manner are not conducive to attracting a husband. Her mam said she could be pretty, if she tried, with her clear hazel eyes and full set of teeth. And if she brushed her hair now and then. Her mam won't let Mary sell her hair; says she needs it to keep warm when out fossil hunting. Where would they be with no fossils to sell?

'Here, Tray!' The dog bounces around Mary's heels, and she continues her walk. A mile and a half of curving coastline lies ahead, which culminates in a headland of rusty coloured sloping cliff face, levelling off to form Golden Cap: the highest point on the coast. Overlooked by the Black Van Cliffs, the shoreline is different here. Four hundred and thirty feet tall, comprising sandwich-like layers of limestone and shale, the cliffs are dark, crumbly and precarious, more so after the storm. Frequent mudslides drag down hundreds of tiny fossils, and Mary picks them like berries. She is cautious, though; beneath the crusty surface, thick mud sucks you under like quicksand. People get stuck, with no choice but to say their prayers, and await the incoming tide and a watery grave.

A shallow wink catches Mary's eye, and she fishes around a nearby rock pool— the ladies love a glittering nugget of fool's gold for their trinket boxes. Scooping away handfuls of mud and water; a jagged edge scratches her arm, and she glimpses the outline of jawbone. So expert is she; she can identify a fossil straight away, even though a partial sighting, but she's unsure about this one. Buried under heavy mud and extending far into the rock, she can't release it on her own. She marks the spot with a pile of shingle, like buried treasure, and crowns it with a pearl-white shell; then, lifting her skirts an inch, she races back to town.

Back along East Cliff, up the steep stone steps and onto Church Street. In the distance, the protective arm of the Cobb curls around two fishing boats in the harbour, taking shelter from the night's storm. Gulls circle above, on the lookout for easy pickings from the dawn trawlers, their screeches accompanied by the rhythmical tap-tapping of stonecutters dangling from ropes, extracting limestone from the rock ledges. Mary makes her way up the incline and narrow thoroughfare of Broad Street: in mid-season carts and carriages jostle for space with holidaymakers; but it is deserted this morning, apart from several workers heading for the mills dotted along the river Lym.

On the right-hand side, for two hundred yards, the river runs parallel to Cockmoile Square, and residents empty their slops in the fast-running water as it flows down to the sea. At least, with the cooler weather, the foul smell has subsided. In summer, the Square's cramped wooden-framed houses front stalls, selling miniature jugs and tankards marked *Lyme Regis*— souvenirs for the well-to-do, who come to reap the health benefits of sea-air and salt-water. Mary's house, which she shares with her mam, has three floors, including a cellar where she cleans and prepares her fossils. Out front on a long table between two bay windows, she displays and sells them: swirled-ammonites, arrow-shaped belemnites, and seashells of all shapes: coils, cones, flutes—and colours: pinks, creams, stripes. All polished and shining, like jewels. Perfect seaside mementoes.

Mary turns left into Silver Street, with its thatched houses and sloping gardens. Situated at the top, with fantastic views over the town and sea, is her destination: Morley Cottage. A small older woman, wearing a white half-apron, answers the door. The odour of hot coffee and fried bacon exude from within, making Mary's mouth water.

'I want to speak to Miss Elizabeth,' she demands, not at all out of breath by her recent exertions.

'The sisters are having breakfast.' The housekeeper's reply is just as firm. She regards Mary as an undesirable specimen and makes her repeat everything twice because of the 'odd way she talks', meaning her broad West Country accent.

'Please, Mrs Burrows. It's important.' Mary pokes a sodden toecap in the doorway. The dislike is mutual; the old woman is a servant, but she acts like one of them with her airs and graces.

'I will inform Miss Elizabeth. Wait here.' The housekeeper backs down, worried in case Mary bursts in, trailing mud and a stench of seaweed that smells like cheap scent sold on the Square.

'Whatever is the matter, Mary?' Elizabeth's soft brown eyes and concerned expression quells the hostile feeling, inspired by the haughty housekeeper. Elizabeth's hair, pinned-back with a tortoise-shell comb, is greying at the temples, and the care-lines on her brow and around her mouth show the onset of middle-age. Twenty years older than Mary, she is the eldest daughter of a recently deceased solicitor. Yet, despite differences in age and social class, she and Mary found friendship through their mutual interest in fossils. Elizabeth, a keen collector of fish fossils, displays her exhibits in glass cabinets throughout the cottage. When she first arrived in Lyme two years ago, Mary showed her where to find the best ones; in return, Elizabeth taught Mary how to record and make labels for her own specimens. They have spent numerous hours together, walking the seashore: a conducive arrangement as it doesn't do for respectable ladies to roam about unchaperoned.

'I've found another monster,' Mary blurts, impatient to return to the treasure. 'Can't shift it on me own.'

Elizabeth trusts Mary's knowledge, and judging by her flushed face and shining eyes, the discovery is significant. She grabs her tool bag and accompanies Mary back to the beach.

'It's different from what I found before.' Mary frowns at the exposed fossilised skull and vertebrae. She can usually estimate the length of a creature by the small bones at the base of the neck, but this one confounds her. 'It's about nine feet long. But the head is only five inches.'

'Oh, Mary. It's wonderful. You may have found a new genus.' Elizabeth runs her fingers over the rough nodules, tracing the outline of the strange creature.

'We must release them parts what's showing, or else the sea will take them by tomorrow.' Mary digs with her trowel, pausing now and then to chip away flakes of rock, keeping an anxious eye on the cliffs above. Time is short, with high tide barely three hours away; she knows by instinct.

Unable to make much progress between them, Elizabeth hurries back to the harbour to ask the stonecutters for assistance. She lures two away with promise of a shilling each, although they are also inquisitive about Mary's latest find. All the locals know about her childhood discovery of the Ichthyosaurs. They used to think her strange and mysterious, like the creatures she hunted. She was different, for sure. But their attitude changed, as influential scientists and geologists visited Lyme wanting to meet her, examine her fossils and inspect the cliffs. They lodge in the seaside hotels with their wives and dine in the pubs and restaurants. Mary brings the town much-needed new business.

Removing his cap, heavy with limestone dust, a stonecutter peers into the murky rock pool. 'What you found this time, Miss? A croc or another sea monster?'

'I'm not sure.' Mary glances at the encroaching tide and puts them to work straight away. 'Good, you've brought your shovels and picks. We don't have much time. Be careful. I don't want it damaged.'

Under Mary's instruction, they free as much fossil as possible without the aid of heavy machinery, until the incoming tide forces them to abandon the task. Then they tie the heavy slabs of rock onto wooden boards and transport them back to her cellar in Cockmoile Square.

Mary cleans the slabs with white vinegar, sandpaper, and a soft-bristled brush, removing dirt and debris to reveal delicate webs of canals that formed the fossil's bone structure. She works throughout the night and the following days. Mam brings a mug of scalding tea every few hours, which Mary grips to warm her numb fingers and sips to unclog her dust-lined throat.

The tart acidic fumes make Mam's eyes water, and she rattles and coughs in the thick air. She once hated the fossils because of the constant grey dust that clings to everything, but more so because they gave her husband an excuse to escape the cries of hungry children and the unhealthy stink of the cramped Square. He'd disappear all day, even on Sundays when decent folk went to church, and he combed the beaches and cliffs in all weathers, breathing the fresh sea air, eyes stretched over the vast expanse of sea. When he died, Mam, previously adverse, now encouraged Mary to hunt fossils, warning that the workhouse loomed, and they would never see each other again.

Mary finally lays out the slabs on the floor and fits them together like a jigsaw puzzle: lizard's head, crocodile teeth, serpent's neck and paddles like a whale—the creature *is* unlike anything she has seen before. It is extraordinary. She draws a pen and ink sketch and posts it with a letter to William Buckland, an old acquaintance, telling him of her latest discovery. She has known Buckland since childhood, when he and his father also collected fossils along the Dorset coast. He later studied mineralogy at Oxford and is nowadays a clergyman. Despite differences in social class, as with Elizabeth, Mary's friendship with him endured: a bond formed through their shared interest. Buckland's money and resources will enable the release of the remainder of the fossil from the cliff. And he will find a buyer.

Three months later

'A fake!' Mary screws up Buckland's letter and catapults it across the cellar floor.

Mam gasps and shakes her head in disbelief.

Mary wipes away her tears with an angry sweep of her hand. 'I know more about the creatures than they do, despite all their schooling. It's me what finds them. But they make out it's all down to them. So, they take the credit and even name my monsters after themselves.'

In the unexpected correspondence, Buckland 'regretfully' informs Mary that the authenticity of her latest discovery is under dispute. On arrival in London, it was examined by William Conybere, the leading authority on Ichthyosaurs and Plesiosaurs, who was looking forward to presenting it to the Geological Society. However, Georges Cuvier, the eminent French anatomist, after seeing Mary's drawing, suspects the fossil is fake, produced by combining bones from other specimens. Following his critique, a thorough scientific investigation into the fossil's authenticity ensues.

Mary welcomed the gentlemen into her little world, gave her knowledge and experience without payment, showed them the best places, guided them along the dangerous cliff paths, and even found them specific specimens. They came and picked her brains. Now they doubt her integrity and question her knowledge. Moreover, if they deem the fossil a fake, her reputation will be ruined and her business in disrepute. Although mid-morning, Mary retires to bed, not having the heart to search for any more fossils.

Elizabeth calls around Cockmoile Square, enquiring after her friend, but Mary refuses to see her. Elizabeth is one of them. She can't trust her. Mam brings Mary a comforting cup of hot tea, and a bowl of water for faithful Tray, curled-up beside.

'Them scientists will see the truth, if they are as smart as they think they are,' she tells her daughter. 'They will realise what you have found for them.' Her mam believes Mary is honest and clever, and she knows what she's talking about when it comes to her fossils.

After lengthy prevarication, the scientists do decide the fossil is authentic and an entirely new genus, after all. Conybere presents it to the Geological Society to rapturous applause and a standing ovation, and, at the end, he officially names the creature Plesiosaurus Giganteus. Mary receives payment of one hundred pounds.

'I'll treat us both to a nice new dress, Mam. And I'll buy me best boy, Tray, a juicy mutton shank.' She rubs the dog's ears. 'I've got plans, Mam. About time we moved out of this stinking shack into somewhere more befitting. Maybe one of them houses on the hill. I want to expand the shop— "The Fossil Depot" I'll name it. Not short of customers now, are we?'

Fuelled by controversy and publicity over the new specimen, Mary's reputation has spread. Scientists worldwide correspond with her and visit Lyme to see where she discovered Plesiosaurus Giganteus. She enjoys showing off to these distinguished gentlemen, proud to call them friends. Although, she finds it annoying how they receive credit for her discoveries, write about them in scientific journals, and present them to the Geological Society while not allowing her entry based on her sex. However, she is contributing to something bigger: there is talk of evolution, of creatures becoming extinct and changing into another form. In the Bible, the Creation story describes how God made the earth in six days; in a more recent 'realistic' account, Bishop Ussher calculated the dates in Genesis to claim that the world is 6,000 years old. But the fossils are evidently much older than that. They are frightening for many, challenging Scripture, and long-held Christian beliefs. People need time to get used to it.

Mary's destiny is to walk the seashore and the cliff paths, earning a meagre living from the fossils she finds and sells; at least they put food on the table and make her life more bearable, and she must be content with that. Buried in time, her story will be forgotten. But in years to come, her achievements may be unearthed and, like her own discoveries, valued as part of the ongoing history of life on earth.

Workhouse Child

Her father disappeared into thin air, and it was a blessed relief because he took with him his fists and his drinking. But he left them with no money and not a crumb in sight. So, her mam weeps on the dreaded Union steps, one hand clutching a tiny bundle against her chest, the other outstretched to the child who did her best to keep up.

'Be a good girl,' her mam says. 'They'll look after us here.'

'You're in luck; there's a couple of empty beds.' The warden ushers them in opposite directions.

An old crone, bent-backed and toothless, wearing a blue and white striped cotton gown under a white apron and shawl, takes charge of the child.

'This way, dear.' She leads the way down a long white corridor with enormous windows, set high up so the inmates can't look out.

Blinded by the brightness, the child trips over a young woman scrubbing the floor.

'Aw, poor love.' The young woman grins black teeth. She wears a similar uniform as the crone, but her gown has yellow and black stripes, indicative of her shame. Her bastard baby, swaddled in rags, grizzles two hundred yards away in a cold room they call the nursery.

The crone deposits the child in a square brick chamber containing two stone baths. A stern, stout figure, wearing a frilly cap and white apron, emerges out of the steam.

'That's Matron,' the crone whispers. 'Do what she says, or there'll be hell to pay.'

'Let's have you out of them mucky rags, then.' Matron looks the child up and down like a lamb at market. But unlike a lamb, this one's worth nought; moreover, a burden to society. She points to the scalding water and proceeds to scrub the tender body, peering into every orifice with apprehension, as if evil lurks within. Once deemed free of contagion, Matron hands the child a regulation brown dress, white pinafore, and a long white nightdress. 'You can have your old rags back when you leave. If you leave.'

She marches the child back out into the corridor to another room where compartmentalised wooden boxes, more like coffins than beds, edge long dark walls.

'You will sleep here.' Matron whips the end of one with her cane, making the child flinch. 'Put your nightdress under the blanket. We like to keep things nice and tidy.' A folded nightdress already in place signifies the child will share with a stranger.

Twenty-two inches above the bed, a narrow strip of wood with long nails protruding at twenty-two-inch intervals, runs the length of the room. 'You can hang your clothes, 'ere.' Matron flogs the nail, making the child jump again. 'Lucky, you got here in time for supper. I'll send one of them to fetch you. Make yourself at home.' And Matron marches out, leaving the child alone.

Dull sunlight peers through a high barred window, illuminating three huge plaques hanging on the wall: each a variation on the benevolence of the Heavenly Father.

GOD IS GOOD_ GOD IS JUST_ GOD IS LOVE

The child perches on the end of the makeshift bed, legs dangling over the abyss, and wonders about her mam.

They peel the limp bundle from her mam's chest like drowned vermin and drop it in a crate. Like all new inmates, they examine and issue her mam a uniform, according to status. But because of her ill-health, they send her to the infirmary rather than the workhouse.

On Sunday, they let her child visit her. Bedridden and weak, she manages a faint smile because, despite her misfortunes, at least her daughter is safe.

'Be a good girl, Lucy,' she says. 'They'll look after you, here.'

'Your mam's passed on, child,' Matron says.

A brown skinny rat slinks under the gate and scuttles elsewhere. Rhythmic thuds break the silence as paupers in secluded cells wield heavy hammers, shattering rocks into smithereens for the sake of a paltry meal and a sheltered sleep. A queue of children creeps round the yard, beneath the high windows of the long corridor, past the washroom with two tin buckets, past the bakery where lingerers bathe in heat wafting out from the ovens, and along the sixteen-foot-high wall that separates them from the men. Two boys, the spirit of youth not yet suppressed, poke protruding ribs and snag thin hair, while keeping a wary eye on the tower for fear the Master watches from above.

A delicious odour of warm, yeasty buns permeates the cold air, making tummies ache and dry mouths drool. The children wait their turn. Some peel the sugar cross off the top and lay it on their tongue, like the Eucharist, the dissolving sweetness resurrecting dormant taste buds. Others wolf it down with bulging cheeks and muffled moans of ecstasy. How will the child eat hers? She might pluck the wizened black dots and save the rest for later. Dizzy with hunger and expectation, she holds out her palm, anticipating a tasty warm pad. But the elder girl in charge of the basket holds out her hand in cruel mimicry.

'A penny!'

Empty-handed, the child runs to the dormitory, falls on her wooden bed and sobs.

A solemn gong announces dinner. She is not hungry, but fear of being late makes her move. Taking her place among the rows of paupers, malingerers, and wretches, she faces front while the Master leads Grace.

'Suffering, sacrifice and salvation,' he hisses. 'Remember Jesus Christ and what he did for us on this holiest of Holy Days. Let us give thanks to our Heavenly Father and our generous benefactors for their gracious bounty. Amen.'

'Amen,' the inmates echo. Scoffing commences, then the scraping of plates and groans of dissatisfaction: a clan of starved dispossessed.

Bread clags the child's mouth, and the cheese stinks like the rat pissed on it before deserting: a disgusted memento of slim pickings. But she prefers it to the breakfast of cloudy water, which reminds her of the wall-hanging paste her father once chucked up the wall. She swallows the bread with a swig of tepid water in case Matron thinks her an ungrateful wretch.

Flexing his cane, the Master patrols the perimeter, alert for wayward souls. After dinner, he tests it on the two delinquent boys with a public flogging on the backside: a necessary deterrent for those whose baser instincts needs quelling. But there are worse punishments.

Four more hours work follows dinner. The child joins two other girls in the kitchen where they collect their scrubbing brushes, and buckets of warm water and washing soda.

'You must earn your keep,' Matron says. 'As do we all.'

The children clear the tables, keeping an eye out for leftovers; unlikely, as fights break out over crusts of already chewed bread; then they scrub the flagstone floor. This is their assigned duty after every meal; not their only duty, though: they sweep and scrub throughout the day—every day of every year. Three waifs, blown hither and thither on the winds of fate. Identical to the disinterested observer**,** but each has their own tragic tale:

Child One scrubs with dreadful imagination. Fingertips trace cracks and joints and test the depths of dark puddles. A minuscule woman with two microscopic children trek across barren terrain, negotiate hills and valleys, ford monster-infested rivers, hoping journey's end will reward them with shelter, warmth, and food—basic human needs. A crumb bullet pierces her flesh. Her knees and hands are red-raw, but she prefers it to picking that stinking rope for hours on end.

Child Two never looks up, never talks, just scrubs. The vigour of her scrubbing implies a conscientious and methodical worker, but she is plain angry. She is better than this. Better than them all. Her father farmed his own land, but the gentry stole it. He sold his horse and tools to feed his family; until, destitute and desperate, he finally begged the local authorities for help.

At least her mother and father are close. She sees them every other Sunday. 'I'll soon be back on me feet, love,' her father says. 'Next season, we'll be out of here, I promise.' But the seasons pass, and still she scrubs.

Child Three scrubs like it makes no difference. She was born here, but she knows life is just as terrible outside. Her mam was a scullery maid in a grand house, for a proper Lord and Lady. She fell pregnant, and they got rid of her before she started showing. She reared her bastard baby on stories about how the upper class take whatever they fancy, regardless.

'We're practising for when they get us proper jobs,' Child Three tells the other two. 'Because that's what we'll do: make things nice and clean for them what's got plenty.' She pinches the end of her nose and sticks it in the air, like they smell bad. Then, seeing Matron watching, she scrubs with more effort; she's felt that cane sting her back many times.

Matron looms, crushing them with the force of her presence. 'The Master has something important to say,' she speaks at last and points her cane at Child One, our child.

The red-faced gentleman sits behind a huge mahogany desk in his office at the top of the tall tower. His upstanding starched collar hides among the folds of his double chin, and the ends of his white knotted bow tie droop like sad angel's wings. Because of his overdoing luncheon, he has unbuttoned the bottom button of his waistcoat, permitting his ample belly to expand unrestricted. On his right-hand side, a be-whiskered young man, wearing a plain suit, studies a thick ledger and scratches dates and numbers with a black goose quill.

A hard knock on the door prompts the red-faced gentleman to button-up and rearrange his posture, ready for business.

'EnTER.' He pronounces the last syllable with a guttural forcefulness, expected of the Master of the institution.

Matron enters with a servile nod and pushes the child forward with her palm.

'Lucy Luck, Sir.'

The child looks at the floor.

'And what are your observations, Matron?'

'Oh, she's a good girl, Sir. Never says a word. Does what she's told and works like most of them. And she does her lessons, but not very smart.'

The Master turns to the be-whiskered young man. 'And how much is the child costing us, Mr Pryce?'

'Case 118, Sir.' Pryce consults his notes. 'Admitted 25th November 1837, aged six, with mother and baby. All in emaciated condition. Baby dead on arrival. The mother was admitted to the infirmary with chronic bronchitis and a weak heart. Died, three days later. Bodies of mother and baby were sent for dissection.' He pauses, takes a breath, and fiddles with his ledger. 'Regarding dietary, Sir. I have calculated, thus.' He hands the Master a list of expenses:

Daily
Breakfast: 1/2pt gruel, 4oz bread
Dinner: 4oz bread, 1oz cheese
Supper: 4oz bread, 1oz cheese
Tuesday Dinner: 4oz meat, 1/2lb potatoes
Saturday Dinner: 1/4lb bacon
Cost per week: 2/3d
Cost per year: £5 17/
Total Cost: £13 2/4d

'Although, total cost is actually less than stipulated, as her rations were reduced due to wastage.' Pryce runs his finger down the page, and, with a delicate cough, clears his throat and resumes his oration. 'Punishment: none recorded.' He raises an eyebrow to Matron, who, arms folded, nods in affirmation. 'Medical treatment: three days in the infirmary due to fainting fits; another two days with a nasty cough; and a consultation for bleeding fingers.' He scours the page for extra costs, although finds none. 'We had hoped to be renumerated with her picking oakum, sir. But the child's skin and respiratory were so adversely affected, we put her on domestic duties instead, which she carries out well enough, or so I'm informed.' He looks again at Matron, who again nods in affirmation.

With gusto, the clerk ends his recitation, 'The child has been with us two years, three months and four days.' And he shuts the ledger with a self-approving snap.

The Master looks at the child for the first time and beckons her forward with a podgy forefinger. 'Not very robust is she, Matron?' he says, taking in the pronounced cheekbones, sunken eyes, and over-sized uniform, looking like it still hangs on that nail.

'Well, Sir, she weren't eating. But I threatened her with the dark hole, which encouraged her appetite somewhat.'

The Master leans forward and addresses the child, not unkindly. 'Today is your birthday, my dear; time you were off our hands. And with the good Lord's grace, your fortunes may improve.' He grimaces, baring yellow tombstone teeth in what he considers an expression of fatherly benevolence. 'We have obtained you a placement with the widow, Mrs Kindly: an old woman, grateful for company. She will fatten you up.' He consults Mr Pryce's sheet of paper. 'And henceforth, you will learn a trade. We have apprenticed you at the mill as a power-loom weaver. Your pay will go towards your bed and keep.' His voice drops an octave, and he continues in a tone that sounds like utmost sincerity. 'Be a good girl. Work hard and pray for those who feed and care for you.' He flicks his hand towards the door. 'Right, off you go, child.'

He leans back in his chair with a satisfied grunt. 'And what have we next on today's agenda, Mr Pryce?' he enquires of the be-whiskered young man on his right-hand side.

Strike

Mabel vomits into a bucket at the side of the bed, leaving long strands of brown hair stuck to the pillow. She resists the urge to wretch again and examines the meagre ejections of her stomach: white watery potato and orange carrot specks— remnants of last night's dinner— garnished with translucent-yellow, bitter-tasting bile.

'Hurry up, love. It's half-past-five,' her mam shouts from the kitchen.

Mabel straightens her hair with her fingers—best not to comb through—and pulls on her dress.

'Come on, sleepy head. Fancy another 5d fine?' Sarah, her sister, the eldest at nineteen, waits by the front door.

'It's alright for you, bossy boots, out the way in that office.' Mabel fastens her jute work apron and grabs a slice of bread and butter off the table. The three women leave the house together.

'Gawd, what a stench.' Mabel wafts her hand to divert the pungent mix of rotting household waste dumped in the middle of the road and the stench of the river Lea drifting from a mile away.

Other early risers tumble out of terraced houses, lining the narrow street. Men mostly, pulling caps over bent heads, thin fags dangling from dry lips, heading for the docks, hopeful of a day's work. Sarah spots Nora walking down Mile End Road, waves and waits for her to catch up. Nora smiles, then grimaces and holds the side of her face.

'Are you alright, love?' Sarah asks her friend.

'It's me tooth.' Nora moves her hand, revealing her flushed and lopsided left cheek. 'I'll be alright. Don't tell anyone, Sarah, promise.' Nora's mam would fret and complain about how she would rather starve in Ireland than die in that bloody poisonous factory. Besides, if she takes a sick day, they might not have her back, and her family needs her wages, more so since her dad up and left.

'Well, tell us if it gets worse. Don't suffer in silence.' Sarah rubs her arm in sympathy.

They turn right into Bow Road and walk past a church with a stubby bell tower and a large blue clock face. A little late this morning, thanks to Mabel, they adjust their pace accordingly. Time is money. The stony gaze of a marble gentleman traces their steps from within the churchyard. He is splendidly attired in a full-skirted frock coat, bow tie and a waistcoat, with a watch chain hanging from the pocket. His countenance severe, his right hand is outstretched, as if addressing them.

'Good mornin', Mr Gladstone.' Mabel bobs a curtsey.

In the distance, a gigantic poster on the end-terrace proclaims in bold black letters:

BRYMAY SAFETY MATCHES

The women take a left turn onto Fairfield Road, where the Bryant and May Match Factory stretches the length of the street. Covering six acres, the factory is the biggest in London. Rising from the centre of the complex, a 200-foot-high water tower is visible for miles: a helpful landmark for unlucky souls who lose their way in the East End's myriad of winding streets and back alleys. With its high red-brick wall and imposing iron gates, the destitute often mistake the Bryant and May Match Factory for the local workhouse, although some say you have a better chance of surviving the workhouse. If such discrepancy arises, a large concrete plaque, inlaid in the brickwork by the gates, is embossed with a fancy *B&M*. On the other side of the wall, behind a stone-paved forecourt, stands a three-storey building with equidistant elongated windows. Above the entrance, a decorative arch bears a gigantic circular white clock with black Roman numerals.

'Watch where you put your feet.' Sarah skips over a damp patch on the ground. 'Rosie Donovan puked her guts up here yesterday.' When Sarah started work at the factory five years ago, she thought the fluorescent pools of vomit outside the factory gates amusing, and the men who glow green like Martians in the dark winter evenings. She thinks differently now.

Last-minute arrivals rush through the entrance with one eye on the clock and utter brisk greetings.

'Mornin' Sarah.'

'Mornin' Alice. How's your mam?'

'Better, since she left work.'

'Maeve, when's your gran's funeral?'

'The wake's on Saturday. Coming to see her off?'

'We'll try. One of the best, your gran.'

'Hey, Sarah, I've got some beautiful new feathers. Will make a lovely hat.'

'I'll nip round soon, love.' Sarah closes the front door behind them. 'Twelve hours to go. See you at break time, Mam.' She scrubs Mabel's head with affection, uprooting several more hairs, and heads down the corridor towards the offices.

The others go through another door leading to the massive factory floor. Mam takes her place by the cutting machine, where two women are hard at work already. Like Mam, they are on piecework. Their job involves slicing the long, thin pine sticks in half after being dipped and both ends have tiny bright red heads. They earn 23/4d for three gross boxes. Nora and Mabel's workbench is further down. They both pack the full matchboxes into frames: Nora earns 1s 9d per dozen boxes; as Mabel is only fourteen years old, she earns a weekly wage of 4s. The match workers comprise primarily women and girls, ages ranging from fourteen upwards, although a few men dip the sticks into huge chemical vats. Many are Irish immigrants, like Nora's family. Unskilled in any trade, they came to England hungry and desperate to earn a living. A generation later, they are still hungry and desperate. Except for the noise of machinery and the familiar coughing, the factory floor is silent—the 3d fine curbs idle chatter. It took a while, but Mabel finally learnt to keep her mouth shut.

At one o'clock, the foreman blows his whistle for break time, and Sarah joins the others for lunch at Mam's cutting machine. Mam shifts her tools off the workbench and lays out half a dozen slices of bread and butter and three jars of cold tea.

'Aw, what's that awful stink?' Mabel peers under the bench, pinching her nose, half-expecting a decomposing rat.

'Shush. It's poor Sam.' Mam nods at a man sitting four yards away, who has climbed down the ladder from the vats to eat his lunch. Shoulders slumped, sucking on a piece of dry bread, his profile shows his misshapen jawline, discoloured green and black. 'The phossy jaw,' Mam whispers. 'Brimstone in the chemicals what causes it.'

Mabel dips her bread in cold tea and feels the back of her head, checking her hair.

The foreman blows his whistle, again. 'Right, back to work, you lot.' A man of variable temper, prone to clouting the women, the management gave him total control, including punishment and dishing out fines. The women try not to cross him.

Nora can fill three frames an hour on a good shift, but weak and exhausted from her nagging tooth, she won't hit her target today. Hands shaking, she picks up her full frame and heads for the stairs leading to the second floor, where she will swap it for an empty one. She stumbles on the first step, and a hundred matchboxes scatter across the floor, spilling their contents.

'You dozy cow.' The foreman takes a swipe. 'That will cost you sixpence. Get to my office.'

Ten minutes later, Nora leans against the exit, forcing her aching arms into her coat. Folks used to call her pretty, but not these days with her yellow complexion, swollen face, and thinning hair. Sarah reappears and helps her.

'He says she can't come back till she's had the tooth pulled,' Sarah shouts over to her mam. 'She nearly passed out. I'm taking her home. I'll nip and put our dinner on after.' Mam waves in affirmation. 'Here, lean on me, love.' Sarah puts her arm around Nora's thin waist and leads her out of the factory.

Sarah sits at the kitchen table, reading the newspaper: "A woman was assaulted in Whitechapel. A man pulled a knife out of his pocket and stabbed her in the legs and lower abdomen. She was admitted to the workhouse infirmary. Another woman, a dressmaker, named Ada, of 11 Maidman Street, Mile End, was viciously attacked at home. A man with a fair moustache and a sunburnt face knocked on the door and threatened to kill her if she didn't give him some money. When she refused, he stabbed her in the throat with a knife. Her screams disturbed her neighbours upstairs. The hallway was a bloodbath."

Sarah recognises the woman's name. She was a prostitute, though, not a dressmaker. Attacks on women are common, but this one is too close to home. Not wanting to dwell on the murdering maniac at large in her neighbourhood, Sarah quickly turns the page and reads the next headline: "Trouble at the London Dockyard. Another dispute over money. A fight broke out, and the police were called."

Mam's voice outside, high-pitched, and excited, disturbs Sarah's reading. 'Well, let's hope she's as good as her word. Fingers crossed. See you tomorrow, Alice love.'

Mam and Mabel spill into the house. 'Put the kettle on, our Sarah. I'm parched.' Mam kicks her shoes into the corner.

'What's happened? Why are you so late, Mam?' Sarah places two plates of stone-cold potato and cabbage on the table, knowing they are hungry and will eat it anyway.

'This woman was standing by the factory gates when we finished work. She asked us all sorts.'

'Who was she, Mam?'

'Annie Besant, she said her name is. She's writing a report about us match workers for her newspaper.'

'I've heard of her.' Sarah taps the table, thinking. 'She writes about poor folk, orphans, prostitutes, and the like.'

'Well, she's doing a piece on us now. A beautiful black dress, she was wearing, with lace down the front. And a decent pair of heels. Posh voice with a kind face and sad eyes. I told her we hate the bloody factory and only work there because we can't do anything else; and about how the management takes money off us, just for talking and dropping a few lucifers. All they care about is their precious lucifers. I told her, didn't I, Mabel?'

'You did, Mam. Hope we don't get into trouble.'

'To hell with them. And I told Mrs Besant about poor Nora.' Mam stuffs a spoonful of potato in her mouth, then spits it out with years of pent-up bitterness. 'Things have always been bad, though. That statue of Mr Gladstone, Mr Bryant stopped a shilling out of the workers' wages and gave them half a day's holiday to pay for it. The workers didn't want no holiday or no statue. They just wanted their pay. Your grandma, God rest her soul, said they all went to the unveiling and threw stones and bricks, and when the nobs had gone, they cut themselves with knives and let the blood trickle down the marble. You can still see the blemishes. Nah, they don't care about us. Lucifers and money are all they care about.'

They hear nothing more from Mrs Besant over the next week and suppose she is just another middle-class do-gooder out to satisfy her curiosity. However, one evening after work, Alice calls round no. 9 Mile End Road, bringing with her the latest edition of *The Link* newspaper.

'Annie Besant's newspaper,' she says, handing it over.

'Sarah, come and have a look, love,' Mam calls. 'My eyes ain't so good.'

On the front page below the title is a quotation by Victor Hugo: *I will speak for the dumb. I will speak of the small to the great and the feeble to the strong. I will speak for all the despairing ones.*

'That's us alright,' Mam says. 'Been despairing all me life.'

Sarah reads aloud, 'White Slavery in London, the article's called.'

'It's true, we are slaves.' Mam's gearing up for another outburst.

'Shush, let me read it.' Sarah skims through and summarises the article for her eager listeners: 'At a meeting of the Fabian Society, Mrs Bessant was horrified when she heard about the low pay and diabolical working conditions of the workers at the Bryant and May match factory. Particularly as the latest financial report reveals the business is paying out 23% dividends to shareholders.'

'Oh, my Lord. They are getting rich while we starve,' Mam says.

'Listen! Mrs Besant interviewed the match workers to find out for herself.' Sarah nods. 'This is where you come in, Mam. Well, she doesn't mention any names. Then she goes on about low pay, long hours, unfair fines, and debilitating health conditions.'

'Just like I told her,' Mam says. 'Things will change, now. Won't they, Sarah?'

'We'll see, Mam. We'll see.' Sarah knew the match workers tried to change things years ago, before her time. But it came to nothing.

The following day, copies of the newspaper containing the damning article fly around the factory.

'Mr Bryant wants a word with you two in the office.' The foreman stabs a forefinger at Mam and Mabel. Mr Bryant rarely visits the factory; besides being a busy businessman, he also supports the Liberal Party.

'See what the old devil has to say, shall we?' Mam casts a triumphant glance over her shoulder as the foreman escorts them to the office.

The eyes of the match workers flit towards the office door, and Sarah lingers by the cutting frame, pretending to scribble in a ledger. When Mam and Mabel finally emerge, it is not the sight everyone was hoping for. Mabel is sobbing, and Mam is fit to burst.

'Mr Bryant sacked us. The foreman saw us talking to Mrs Besant,' she says. 'He wants us to sign a statement saying everything in the newspaper is all lies and that we are happy with working conditions. No way, I says. It's a living hell, truth be told. Lucifers, brimstone, and all.'

Shouts of anger drown out sighs and moans of disappointment.

'The old beggar!'

'He can't get away with it, can he?'

Sarah stands next to Mam and puts her arm around Mabel. She is angry, too: not a rash, fiery anger like Mam's, but a calm, suppressed anger that has been fermenting for five years as she witnessed her family and friends struck down by ill-health and overwork. She remembers her grandma's words when she started work: *Always hold your head up, Sarah. You are as good as anyone.* Sarah earned a promotion to patents last year, but these women are her friends, and she can't stand back and watch them being exploited to death any longer. She steps forward and addresses them in a loud, clear voice.

'This job is killing us. And for what? We don't get paid enough for what we do. And they rob half of it back with their fines. They are getting rich from our sweat and blood. Look, it says so here, in black and white.' She waves the newspaper in the air, like a flag of revolt. 'We are not lifting another finger until conditions improve. People know about us now. Important people like Mrs Besant. We ain't working in this hell hole a minute longer!'

Sarah, Mam, Mabel, and their friends walk out, having done no work. Many other match workers follow; Sarah's words and Mrs Besant's article have struck a chord. By the end of the day, the factory has ceased production: 1,500 match workers refuse to work.

The angry footsteps of one hundred women and girls reverberate through London's East End. They march up Bow Road, down Mile End and Fleet

Street and on to Bouverie Street, where they arrive at the press offices of *The Link* newspaper. Although brave in taking a stand against the factory owners, the strikers don't have a penny to live off. Sarah asks if they may please speak to Mrs Besant. Mrs Besant invites three inside, and Sarah takes with her Mam and Alice.

The others wait in the street: young girls with younger mouths to feed, women whose husbands are out of work, and women whose husbands have deserted them. For many, the workhouse calls, but they would rather die than return to work. Excited and determined, they stand close, bolstering each other, making plans.

'Old Bryant soon changed his tune when we all walked out, didn't he? He even offered Mabel and her mam their jobs back.'

'But we want more than that, like Sarah said.'

'We must stick together. Hit Bryant and May where it hurts: in their bleedin' pockets.'

After an hour, Sarah and the others return.

'Shush quiet, everyone.'

Standing on the steps of the press office, Sarah addresses the match workers.

'Mrs Besant was shocked when I told her we left our jobs and have no means of support. For a minute, I thought she would send us back to the factory. But no, she will help us!'

Jubilant cheers from the match workers.

'Mrs Besant will report in her newspaper about us being on strike and tell folks how terrible Bryant and May treat us. She will also help us set up a strike fund to stop us from starving. And we are going to form a union of women matchmakers: the union will make us strong. Right, we need to organise. Go home, everyone, while we form an action plan.'

The women disperse, going their separate ways for now, but united against Bryant and May.

The match workers vote eight women to lead the strike committee, including Sarah, Mam, and Alice. They appoint Mrs Besant secretary and set up headquarters near the press office, where they hold meetings and allocate the strike fund. The strikers throw themselves into the fight heart and soul; and loud and confident they bring their plight to the consciousness of the masses. Through the London streets, they parade, crying out for support at the injustices of Bryant and May, wielding their colourful home-made banners:

SUPPORT THE MATCHGIRLS
WHITE SLAVES

and

OUR FIGHT IS YOUR FIGHT
SUPPORT THE
MATCHGIRLS STRIKE

Mrs Besant's newspaper calls for a boycott of Bryant and May matches, and she enlists the aid of many prominent and well-respected celebrities: William Stead, George Bernard Shaw, and Emmeline Pankhurst, to name a few. The strike hits the headlines of the national press, too, and gains enormous sympathy from the public. Donations flood in. The London Trades Council, which usually reserves support for skilled craftsmen, gives twenty pounds to the strike fund and agrees to act as an intermediary in negotiations between the match workers and Bryant and May. Before long, the strike draws the attention of Parliament, and The House of Commons invites 50 match girls to give testimony in their own words, describing the diabolical working conditions.

After three weeks intense campaigning, Sarah reports back from a meeting between the strike committee and Bryant and May management. Tired and pale, but eyes bright with excitement and hope, she faces 1,500 expectant faces.

'Many folks have stopped buying Bryant and May matches, and

profits are down. The adverse publicity has hit their reputations hard. We have them scared; more so, now Parliament's involved.'

Cheers from the strikers, and a few anxious comments:

'About time, an' all.'

'What did they say?'

Sarah takes a deep breath, raises her arms and screams: 'Well, they agree to ALL our terms!' She waits for the cheers to subside, then counts out the terms on her fingers. 'One, they have abolished the fines. Two, they will build us a proper canteen, away from the factory floor and the chemicals. Three, a full-time doctor and dentist will give us regular check-ups. Four, that foreman no longer has power over us to dish out fines whenever he fancies. And five, we can return to work with no consequences.'

More cheering, but Sarah holds up her hand; she's not quite finished.

'We have gained a glorious victory, but not only for ourselves. We are the first unskilled workers to form a union and achieve our goals, and our victory will inspire other poor souls who work in terrible conditions, like the men on the docks. Let's hope they can come together and fight their employers for a better deal like us.'

Sarah gives a final victorious roar, 'Right, friends, let's go and celebrate. We have won!'

Tintinnabulation

CLANG CLANG CLANG. The sun sulks through the window, casting a dull light over two slight mounds under a heavy patchwork quilt. Annie pokes her nose out of the warm sanctuary, anticipating the nip of morning air. With a quick flick of her arm, she sheds the quilt, then pulls on her clothes. The coarse cloth of her underwear grates her young skin, and her knees momentarily buckle under the weight of her work apron. She tames her long fair hair into a neat, tight bun, accomplished without the aid of her right little finger, which the loom had robbed a month earlier, and grabbing her white mob cap off the end of the bed, she tiptoes across the floorboards. Jessie, age six, her younger sister, still fast asleep, has four more years till she will adopt the same routine.

In the scullery, their mother saws thick slices of bread for breakfast. Bent-backed and red-cheeked, she flashes her daughter a smile. 'Come on, Annie, love. Tea's brewing.'

Annie rubs her bare arms, and the goosebumps recede in the heat emanating from the roaring fire. She looks for her father. There he is, slouched in his armchair by the fender, gnawing on a crust. The fiery flames give him a crimson glow, and the sweat seeps from the crags in his face like soulful tears. She tries to catch his eye, but he looks away; his bewildered expression resembles a tormented demon, tired of the toils of this world and homesick for his own hell. He sighs and scratches his whiskers, trying to solve a riddle, long forgotten. His absences from work are becoming regular. Annie grits her teeth and purses her lips. She resents his selfish moodiness and emotional detachment and longs to kick him into action. *'Get off your lazy arse,'* she wants to yell.

'He'll be alright, love. He just needs a rest.' Her mother puts his apathy down to an unexplained illness.

Is it contagious? Annie wonders because the man next door suffers the same ailment.

Her dad wheezes and coughs up a globule of green phlegm. He spits into the fire, and it ignites into a cloud of toxic fumes, then sizzles into nothing.

A week-old baby gurgles from a makeshift cot in the corner, and another child toddles across the floor, babbling incoherently, the world still new and appealing. The threadbare rug falls two feet short of the wall, and a splinter in the exposed floorboards impales the child's soft foot. Mam sweeps him up in loving arms, and dangles a picture of baby Jesus, Mary, and Joseph, given out by the vicar at church, to stop the crying. She has subjected all her children to colourful and captivating stories from the Bible: stories of suffering, hope and salvation. They learnt to read by quoting extracts from scripture out loud to the family every Sunday evening.

Annie gulps down the tea, scalding her throat but warming her insides. 'I'll be late home, Mam. Promised Grace I'd go to some meeting after work.'

The door slams on her way out.

Twelve hours after leaving the house, Annie rubs her aching back and stretches her sore fingers. Pulling on her coat, she glances out of the factory window. Weary workers stumble through tall iron gates like over-milked cattle, heads bent, bracing against the evening chill. A young woman looks around, stoops to pick up a shilling glistening in the mud and slips it in her pocket, not believing her luck. In the distance, rows of terraced houses beckon with unfulfilled promises of homely satisfaction. Between the scorched chimney pots, a pale full moon ascends the twilight sky; a bright star follows close behind, winking in the lunar aura.

Annie had noticed posters dotted around the canteen during dinner break, but Votes for Women means nothing to her. She wants to go home and put her feet up, but Grace tugs her sleeve.

'Aw, come on, Annie. You promised. Besides, it'll be fun.'

Annie gives in, and linking arms they head for the canteen.

A dozen factory girls attend the meeting. Some out of curiosity. Some to postpone going home. A few, like Grace, want to know more about the Women's Suffrage Movement. They stand in tired little groups, gossiping about the day's occurrences: Lily is in the family way, again; Evelyn's on the streets, can't pay the rent; the manager has sacked Violet, no one knows why. All the usual.

The room turns silent, and Annie looks towards the door. She recognises the woman from the poster: round handsome face, brunette hair done up in a tight-bun—a few stragglers make a charming contrast with her pale complexion. She wears a long brown skirt and a white silk blouse with a high collar. A sash of three horizontal stripes: purple, white, and green, runs across her breast from right shoulder to left hip. A brown flat-topped peaked bonnet tops off her outfit, reminding Annie of an army Captain she had seen in the penny newspaper.

Another woman follows closely behind, similarly attired, but older and taller, straight-backed with a Sergeant Major demeanour and a no-nonsense expression. She carries a leather attaché case and a pile of leaflets. She takes a rear seat, while the other woman remains standing.

The woman smiles even white teeth and addresses her audience in a low, well-bred voice. 'Good evening, ladies. Thank you so much for coming.'

Her presence fills the room. Her voice fluctuates like the ebb and flow of life itself, and Annie clings to it like a drowning creature. The woman's eyes change colour, chameleon-like, matching every phrase and passionate resolve: purple, white, and green. They grow misty, then flash like beacons on a foggy night, drawing Annie in like a lost soul at sea.

Enthralled, Annie doesn't understand what the woman is talking about, until several words strike home.

'Long hours… low pay… women's rights.'

Annie listens with more intent. Her cheeks flush, her heart races, and her eyes turn misty. She takes a deep breath and nudges her friend.

'Grace, she's talking about us!'

Finally, the woman pleads the factory workers to join the Women's Cause, become trade union members and spread the word amongst their fellow workers. The Sergeant Major steps forward and produces a pencil and paper to jot down names on a roll call of political consciousness.

Grasping her friend's arm, Annie leads her forward. 'Come on. Let's do it.' She is shy and out of her depth, but this is bigger than herself. She must be a part of it.

That night, the woman's words reverberate through Annie's mind, and she lies awake, thinking of all the best things she said. Things about what women can achieve if they stick together and have a say in politics. Things can change.

The sunlight sears through the rags at the window, illuminating two slight mounds under a heavy quilt, and the clang of the factory bell rouses Annie from her dreams. She jumps out of bed, oblivious to the cold air nipping her skin; a fire has ignited in her heart and soul. There is work to do, but a different kind of work. It is another morning, but a bright new day.

One Hand Tied Behind Us

'Move along, Madame.' A huge hairy hand on each of their arms escorts the two ladies from the Grand Hall. Mrs Billington smacks him – actually, smacks him. As a result, within the hour, he has them settled in the cells behind Manchester court charged with obstructing and assaulting a police officer. The authorities have the procedure down to a fine art. The ladies refuse to pay the shilling fine, of course, choosing incarceration for three days, instead.

The cell is small, like a cattle stall with bars, and the stale urine and disinfectant cocktail makes Hannah nauseous. She feels vulnerable without her bloomers, and the prison uniform irritates her skin. But she has stayed in worse places, when between jobs.

'Get your bleedin' hands off.' A scuffle with a male prisoner further down the corridor is followed by a resounding slam.

Hannah sits on the hard bunk and cradles her pounding head in trembling hands. All the ridicule and humiliation and now this: locked up like a common criminal. Perhaps she's not up to it. Perhaps it's not worth it.

Christabel Pankhurst and Annie Kenney, her devoted lieutenant, were the first. Hannah was present at their release: much cheering and flag-waving, like soldiers home from the front. At last, Votes for Women hit the newspaper headlines. Twenty years of peaceful propaganda had not produced such an effect, nor thirty years of patient pleading gone before.

'We shall prevail,' Mrs Pankhurst said. 'We are making history.' Things took a turn after that. The smouldering resentment in women's hearts burst into a flame of revolt.

The prison warden opens a six-inch square hatch and pushes through a beaker. 'Here you are, missus. Don't want you dying on us, though I wouldn't put it past you, just to get in the papers.'

'Thank you.' Hannah sips the water.

He sniffs, making the whiskers of his moustache twitch, rat-like. 'Six more the likes of you arrested today, down in London. Kept banging on the Prime Minister's front door. No. 10 Downing Street, no less.' He shakes his head. 'Dunno what this country is coming to. Madwomen running riot in the streets, doing what the 'ell they like. What must your poor husband and children think?' He slams the hatch shut and marches off down the corridor.

Despite the warden's prevarications, the news comforts Hannah. Sisters in revolt all over the country. Some imprisoned for weeks. Some starving themselves. A warm feeling of solidarity runs through her veins, strengthening her resolve, and she settles down for a long night.

The warden soon returns, swinging his keys like a Wild West sheriff. He unlocks the cell door and drops a bundle of clothes on the floor. 'You are free to go, Madam. Your husband has paid the fine.' He kicks the bundle over to where she sits and smirks. 'Probably wants his dinner.'

'What is the time, please?' Hannah asks, frowning.

He consults his gold pocket watch: his father's watch and his grandfather's before, a true family heirloom. 'Half-past five,' he says. 'You're lucky you've a home to go to. I wouldn't let you in if you were my wife.'

Three hours since her arrest. *Only* three hours. How dare Gibbon? Doesn't he understand what this means to her? To the Cause? Besides, they can't afford the fine.

Hannah's husband waits outside, pacing up and down, stroking his beard. He is wearing the navy-blue suit from the pawnshop—Hannah did an excellent job with the alterations.

'Gibbon!' She glares at him, exasperated.

'I know, love. I know.' He reaches for her hand. 'But I thought of your health, and you ought to be at home with the boy and me.'

He should know better. Disappointed and angry, Hannah strides ahead, leaving him behind.

A wave of workers spill out the factory gates. Several know the thin, stern woman, and her husband, trotting behind, from Labour church.

'Evenin', Mrs Mitchell, Mr Mitchell.' They nod and vanish behind narrow doors of thin terraced houses.

As soon as they arrive home, Hannah disappears into the scullery. Besides herself, her husband, and their son, she has two extra mouths to feed: lodgers taken in for five shillings a week on promise of a clean bed and a decent meal a day. She regards the stove with resentment, tips the lid off a large cast-iron pot and sniffs the contents: left-over stew from the previous day. She throws in a pinch of salt and a sprig of rosemary to liven it up and rubs a spoonful of beef suet into a cupful of flour. Adding a little water, she shapes the mixture into balls, and drops them in the pot, like little bombs. Still smouldering, she remains silent. Other marriages have suffered under the strain, and she needs her husband as an ally. Thankfully, tomorrow is Sunday; they can find common ground at the Labour Church.

Gibbon lies in bed till eight on Sundays, having worked all week at the tailor's shop. Hannah gets up at six, as usual, and begins her daily chores. She lights a fire in the living room and the kitchen stove, puts the kettle on, slices slabs of fresh bread, and fries six rashers of bacon. The latter brings the household to life, and she serves breakfast. After they have eaten, she washes the pots, stokes the oven, and prepares dinner for later. She always ensures a proper roast for Sundays: a 3/4 lb leg of beef or a chicken, if they can afford it; stuffing made with fresh herbs and breadcrumbs; roast potatoes and parsnips; boiled potatoes, carrots or peas; Yorkshire pudding and thick homemade gravy; and a fruit pie and custard for after.

Preparations complete, she hangs up her apron and changes into her best skirt and blouse.

Gibbon, already dressed in his best Sunday suit, trawls through a pile of laundry. 'Have you seen my collar, love?

Hannah searches the washing basket—washday was Tuesday, but she's not had time to put it away. Finding the collar, bright white and stiff as a board, she fastens it for him, and they depart for Labour Church.

It was Gibbon Mitchell who introduced Hannah to socialism. She worked as a seamstress at the time, making wedding dresses. He was an apprentice tailor, and they lodged in the same house. There were grumblings, agitation for shorter working hours, and massive bills appeared, appealing for workers to join the union and demand their rights. Gibbon showed Hannah articles about slums and sweated labour in *The Clarion* newspaper and lent her books about inequalities in the social system. Like him, she joined the Independent Labour Party (ILP); the socialists' maxim: *Not just bread but bread and roses, too'* with its emphasis on culture and community, appealed to them both. Although, their apparent promotion of equality between the sexes was of more interest to Hannah. Since becoming interested in politics, she had noticed the lack of women in power and well-paid jobs: especially in Government, the law, and the medical professions.

With a platform rather than a pulpit, the socialists congregate at Labour church every Sunday to discuss social, political, and religious matters. After Hannah and Gibbon married, he took the role of lecture secretary, which brought them in contact with many well-known speakers from the Labour Movement. Hannah met Doctor and Mrs Emmeline Pankhurst, who lived ten miles away. The Women's Social and Political Union (WSPU) were recruiting women from the ILP, and Mrs Pankhurst invited her to their home in Nelson Street.

'Welcome, Mrs Mitchell. We are so happy you could join us.' Mrs Pankhurst took Hannah's hand and spoke in a deep, serene voice, sensitive to her apparent awkwardness. She wore a long brown skirt and white silk blouse with a high white collar; a broach pinned to her breast, near her heart, comprised little coloured ribbons of purple, white and green. Her brunette hair swirled around her head in a tight plait, like a Grecian Goddess.

Three women leant over a map spread out on a large oak table. One of them stood and, clasping Hannah's hand in a firm handshake, introduced herself as Christabel Pankhurst. Hannah recognised her from the WSPU posters. Christabel was shorter than her mother and wore her hair in a bun; but her handsome, round serious face and her soft brown eyes radiated a similar light.

'We are plotting our Votes for Women campaign, Mrs Mitchell. Do you like our colours? Purple for loyalty, white for purity and green for hope', she said, noticing Hannah staring at her brooch.

'I like them very much', Hannah said.

Christabel introduced the other two women as Annie Kenney and her sister, Jessie—good-looking, well-mannered young women, wearing the same dark-coloured costumes of excellent quality—of similar upbringing to Hannah: working-class and underprivileged with limited schooling, but intelligent with a desire for learning. Hannah glanced around the warm drawing-room, marvelling at the many bookshelves, and imagined the adolescent Pankhurst daughters, studying in the glow of a cosy fire. Conscious of her class difference, Hannah was acutely aware of her own poverty, dowdy clothes, lack of social graces and education. But it didn't seem to matter. United under one cause, the women believed winning the vote was the precursor to the emancipation of *all* women and their broader involvement in society.

Introductions over, the women settled down to discuss the WSPU's intensive campaign tactics, which included distributing handbills, disrupting political meetings and street corner public oration. With a red marker pen, Christabel highlighted significant locations on the map to strategically place her suffragettes and their offensive manoeuvres in the war for the vote. After three thrilling hours, Hannah left the Pankhurst home full of hope, feeling her entire life had led to Votes for Women.

Following Labour Church, the socialist men drift towards the pub, but Gibbon and Hannah go straight home for dinner. As breadwinner and head of household he receives the largest food portions. Hannah saves any leftovers for meals during the week: cold meat for tea, beef dripping for sandwiches he can take to work, and the rest she will fry as 'bubble and squeak.'

Table cleared and dishes washed, she settles down for an afternoon baking for the week ahead, when a knock at the door interrupts her.

'Come in,' she shouts.

Edward Mullins from the Labour Church appears, cap in hand. He wants Hannah's assistance in writing a speech. She is a popular speaker herself, on women's equality—gifted in penning an intellectual and reasoned argument and delivering it in the plainest terms, Mrs Pankhurst said.

'I'm too busy, Edward. Sorry.' Hannah wriggles her flour-covered fingers in his direction and reaches for the kettle. 'But do have a nice cup of tea with Gibbon. He's in the living room, reading the newspaper.' Edward declines, wanting to go home and compose his speech. Hannah sighs and thumps the bread dough. She sometimes regrets having married.

She wanted her own home, but they are still poor, struggling to make ends meet. Her mother must have felt like this. How she hated her.

Married to a sheep farmer with no machinery and little money, her mother's unhappiness intensified with the birth of every child. Hannah and her five siblings suffered her beatings, while her gentle father retreated into the hills with his sheep. Hannah did the chores, while her brothers read books, and while they went to school, her mother sent Hannah away on a dressmaking apprenticeship. When she returned home their antagonism worsened, and, aged 14, Hannah ran away from home. Socialism gave Hannah a theoretical framework to understand her mother's misery and her own lack of education. However, while socialists preach equality, they do not support women's equality with men: socialist men expect Sunday dinners and enormous teas with homemade cakes and pies. They expect their wives to begin where their mothers left off.

Breakfast finished, Gibbon's sandwiches packed, Hannah grabs her hat and coat. This morning, she plans to meet Annie Kenney at Ashton Market ground. Between them, they have already canvassed most of Lancashire.

The market is buzzing when they arrive. Annie borrows a crate from a suffragette sympathiser on a nearby stall, and, standing on it, she flings into the familiar rhetoric:

For the love of justice, home, and the little ones, working women of England, I ask you to stand shoulder to shoulder with us in demanding our political freedom. Remember, those who would be free must strike a blow. We have asked, pleaded, and prayed for over 60 years; now, we must fight.

A passionate and vigorous speaker, Annie's Lancashire accent, as opposed to the well-bred tones of the Pankhurst's, is one with which ordinary women can relate, and her identity as the suffragette mill-girl attracts other working-class women to the cause. Soon a crowd gathers. Some are interested; others come to laugh and scoff.

'Ain't you got anything to do at home? You're giving us proper earache,' a man shouts.

Annie continues, unperturbed, despite jeers from the audience.

'If you were my wife, I'd give you poison', another man shouts.

'And if I were your wife, I'd take it.' This time Annie answers back, and a flurry of laughter ripples through the crowd.

Accustomed to hecklers in varying degrees, the suffragettes are often bombarded with cruel comments, sometimes rotten fruit, and eggs. When things get rough, they beat a hasty retreat and carry on elsewhere. Hannah circulates, handing out leaflets, soliciting new recruits and donations. She avoids the rowdy ones, usually men. More serious interest comes from women: the well-to-do ones sneak money into her hand, others snatch leaflets and stuff them in their pockets to read later.

Around mid-morning, Annie returns to suffragette headquarters in Nelson Street for instructions from Christabel, urgently called to London. Hannah joins Mrs Billington at the church hall in Deansgate, where Winston Churchill gives a speech. They both don disguises in case someone recognises them from the previous incident. Hannah wears a feather hat and a voluminous fur coat; in the pockets, she secretes two banners made of white calico, with the slogan 'VOTES FOR WOMEN' painted on in black enamel. She takes a seat in the audience.

A gentleman in the next seat turns to her. 'I say, do you think that awful Pankhurst woman will join us?'

'Oh, why is she speaking?' Hannah's stomach lurches, and she conceals her face with long feathers.

'She doesn't come for that', the gentleman says. 'Haven't you heard of her mob of madwomen creating havoc and disturbing political meetings?'

Before he can press further, proceedings get underway. The chairman speaks the preliminaries, then Churchill takes the stage. Hannah waits a few minutes, then stands, hoisting a banner above her head.

'Will the Liberal Government give the vote to women?' she roars.

Gasps and groans reverberate through the audience.

'Good heavens!' The gentleman looks at her in horror.

Churchill continues his speech, ignoring Hannah. A man snatches her banner from behind.

On the other side of the hall, Mrs Billigton stands and raises her own banner.

'When will you give women the vote?' she bellows.

Hannah unfurls another banner and joins Mrs Billington in a stereophonic attack.

This time, Churchill stops speaking, and the chairman takes the microphone. 'Ladies, leave the premises at once, or someone will forcibly eject you!'

The women's cries for justice grow louder.

Two men grab Hannah under her arms, half-drag her to the door and throw her into the street. She sprawls to the ground.

Her mother always put a yellow carnation in her father's buttonhole, when he went to vote in town.

'Women don't vote, child. It's just the way it is,' she said, when Hannah asked why she wasn't going with him.

Somehow her mother was complicit in it all: the way she made Hannah do the housework while her brothers went to school; the way she called her father the master; and the way she discreetly disappeared whenever he did business, even though instructing him what to say beforehand.

Hannah asked her uncle the same question.

He liked his niece: a sullen, undernourished, and inquisitive child. He felt sorry for her, having such a hard-hearted mother and gave her books when she cried because her mother wouldn't allow her to go to school.

He explained that because men's work as wage-earners lies outside the home, their needs and outlook on life are more expansive than women's, whose interests are centred on the home and family. Therefore, men have better judgement and can make essential decisions and laws for the common good.

Hannah understood but did not accept male superiority in judgement. Her brothers were not exceptionally bright, and her mother ruled the roost at home.

'Well, I'm going to vote when I grow up,' she told him.

Mrs Billington hits the ground with a thud, joining Hannah in the street.

'Oh, good Lord.' She rubs her shoulder. 'Not as young as I was.'

'At least they didn't call the police this time.' Hannah says thinking of the fine. She stands up and brushes herself off. The war is not over by any means. There is still much to fight for, but she *will* vote one day, of that she is certain. It will be worth it. They are making history.

Know Your Place

Margaret is not pretty and generally referred to as hefty. But there is some benefit in being big, strong, looking older than your age and having size nine feet; it comes in handy for lugging around sacks of coal, for one thing. And she is still growing. She has the appetite of a horse, much to her mam's chagrin as there are five other mouths to feed besides, and in all honesty, she can't wait to see the back of her firstborn because she is eating them out of house and home. So, the minute Margaret turns fifteen, her mam decides she will follow in her footsteps and work in domestic service, which is odd because she raised her on horror stories of being a servant.

'Treat you like a slave, they do. And pay you a pittance for your troubles,' she said. 'Keep you locked up like they own you and spout their morals about decent behaviour, while they swan about doing goodness knows what. I could tell you a tale or two that would make your hair curl. And they feed you the plainest food while they gorge on fancy stuff. Mind, I had my fair share of pickings and a tipple when no one was looking.'

Her mam's incessant griping miraculously changed tune overnight into the virtues of service: 'An opportunity to learn new skills and earn a regular wage. You have a lovely home and can work your way up the ranks to chambermaid, even housekeeper.'

The domestic agency has plenty of vacancies. In fact, they are crying out for dutiful servants. However, Margaret's hatred of all forms of needlework limits her choices. She finally plumps for kitchen maid.

Lady Coulter looks her up and down, like a carthorse at market, while Margaret, shy and self-conscious in such grand surroundings, examines her own enormous size nines. The entrance hall was strange enough, with all the heads and antlers—His Lordship was big in India—but the drawing-room's opulence renders her speechless: reflected flames dance across a lustrous black hearth and lick delicate fine china ornaments on small voluted tables; ancient hereditary landscapes and proud family portraits, set in gold gilt frames, cover diamond patterned emerald green wallpaper; a walnut upright piano gleams quiet in the corner; and a crystal glass chandelier casts a rainbow across the fancy-corniced ceiling.

Margaret's mam does the talking. 'She's not afraid of hard work, Madam.' Spurred on by the desire to secure her daughter a job, she lists the girl's finer points. 'Strong as an ox, and healthy, never a day's illness. Honest as the day is long. She goes to Sunday school and church in the evening. God-fearing Christians, we are.' Although truth be told, they don't fuss about religion. But it's the only time Mam and Mad get a bit of peace, and Sundays generally result in the conception of yet another child.

Lady Coulter nods her head, satisfied. The job is Margaret's at 24 pounds a year, with one afternoon and one evening off a week, plus alternate Sundays.

In the shadows of a magnificent curling row of white regency houses, Margaret pushes a half-empty barrow down Kensington Crescent. She descends a dozen steep steps and arrives at the tradesman's entrance of Parkland House. A young woman wearing a navy-blue uniform, white bibbed apron and frilly cap introduces herself as 'Elsie the housemaid' and leads the way down a long passageway. A putrid smell, reminiscent of the dead pigeon Margaret's dad discovered in their chimney last summer, emanates from a doorway on the right. Pinching her nose, Margaret glances inside. An assortment of game hangs from the rafters—pheasant, partridge, rabbit, and hare—more evidence of His Lordship's penchant for shooting things. On the floor, a ripe head wriggles with life, and Margaret shudders, thinking her job will involve plucking and skinning the poor dead creatures.

A sharp tinkle and another maid darts through a door at the end of the passageway. 'Flamin' hell. Did you see which one, Elsie?' The maid examines eight rows of little bells attached to a board on the wall.

'The drawing room,' Elsie says. 'Best not be tardy again, Gladys, or the old cow will have your guts for garters.'

Margaret follows Elsie through to the servants' hall. The lower half of the walls shine with brown paint, and a bilious green distemper covers the top half; high-up, an oblong barred window lets in a shaft of light, eclipsed at intermittent intervals by parades of legs on the street above. Dull duck-egg blue linoleum covers the floor, with a few shabby rugs scattered willy-nilly. Four misshapen wicker chairs and a long dining table covered in an old oilcloth complete the furnishings. So far, the drab interior belies the marvellous impressions of Margaret's previous visit, and she wonders whether she's in the wrong house.

Elsie takes her through another door and into the kitchen where a magnificent black cast iron range stands across the back wall, shining like new. A perpetual glow of orange and red radiates from the grate, making the room a welcome sanctuary in winter and a living hell in summer. A delicious aroma of fried bacon lingers from breakfast, and Margaret, not having eaten since yesterday's teatime, feels her stomach lurch and groan with desire. 'They'll feed you when you get there,' her mam had assured.

An enormous Welsh dresser, holding 126 pieces of bone china, takes up most of the opposite wall. Numerous pots and pans of various shapes and sizes, glistening in golden copper—a devil to clean—hang from racks, filling every inch of space. Margaret surveys the various cooking paraphernalia, and her heart sinks. But she doesn't know half of it.

In the midst, a diminutive overweight woman, wearing a full-length white apron and a tight mob cap, stands at a vast wooden table, beating the hell out of the contents of an enormous beige earthenware bowl.

'Your new kitchen maid, Mrs Ilford,' Elsie says.

'Well, what's your name, girl?' The woman, red-faced with effort, glances up without breaking rhythm.

'Margaret Longford, Misses.'

'Well, they might change it to something less fancy. You won't see them much, in any case.' By 'them', she means the gentry upstairs. 'You may address me as Cook.' Cook decides to call her Meg because it's less of a mouthful than Margaret, and time is short enough.

'Yes, Cook. Thank you.' Her mam warned her, do as Cook says and treat the other servants with deference, as they can be a bit sensitive.

'Well, show the girl where she will sleep, Elsie,' Cook says, still beating.

They ascend three flights of narrow stairs. Elsie pushes a door ajar on the left-hand side and dull duck-egg blue linoleum gives way to plush ruby red carpet: the threshold to another world. She peeps around the door, checking no one is there.

''Ere, have a quick look.'

Margaret pokes her head through and takes in the sprawling wide corridor, cream walls, and pearl-white doors.

'That's where their bedrooms is.' Elsie closes the door. 'Just so you know. Never go there unless told.'

Continuing the steep climb, they reach a small attic room at the top of the house.

'One hundred and thirty-two steps.' Elsie says, noticing Margaret breathing hard. 'You'll get used to it. You'll have to.' Three single beds are separated by a cupboard and a nightstand, each with an enamel bowl and a water jug. Elsie points under the slanted back wall. 'You can sleep there. Mind your head. The other bed is Gladys's, the under-housemaid. She says little, but we get on fine. You'll be glad of the company. It gets lonely up here.'

Margaret changes into her uniform: blue dress—not the dark navy blue of Elsie's but a lighter blue, designating her lower status—and white apron with long bib straps that fit over her back and button to a belt around her waist. Screwing her long brown hair into a bun, she pins it up and tucks it under her white maid's cap. She has worn her regulation black buckled shoes a week already to break them in; her mam got a voucher from the council. Then, ready for duty, they head back downstairs.

A third of the way down, a young gentleman with fair slicked-back hair wearing a beige tweed suit, leans against the door Elsie previously opened.

'Good morning, ladies.' He touches his brow with a forefinger, ice-blue eyes twinkling. His plummy voice and handsome soft features exude good breeding.

'Mornin', sir,' Elsie says.

He doesn't move, so they breathe in and walk past him sideways. The rough material of his trousers rubs against Margaret's leg.

'That's Master Robert, the old cow's nephew,' Elsie mumbles, when they are out of earshot. 'He stays here, now and then. Wonder why he's hanging around the servant's quarters? He'll cop it if she finds out.'

Back in the kitchen, Cook hands Margaret a list of duties:

Up at 5:30. Clean flue, light fire, blacken grate, clean steel fender and fireirons, polish front door brass, scrub steps, clean boots, and shoes, and lay servants' breakfast.

And after the servants have eaten, she must help Cook prepare breakfast for them upstairs—all before 8:30. Margaret gasps, wondering how on earth it is all possible.

Margaret had thought cleaning easy enough, having done her fair share at home, but they have their own way of doing things here, and there is so much of everything. She spends over an hour just cleaning boots and shoes, and half the morning blackening the hearth in the drawing-room, until Elsie informs her the blackening needs soaking in water overnight. But she most hates polishing the door brass: the door handle, letterbox, top step, and a tremendous gargoyle-shaped-knocker are all brass. She bends over, hoping her flushed reflection will materialise in the top step, but, despite her best efforts, Brasso seeps into cracks and crevices, making everything dull. While vigorously buffing with her yellow duster, passing men whistle and shout lewd comments:

'Fancy a bit of rump for me tea.'

'Come and give this a rub, darlin'.'

Margaret' face burns, and she throws the duster into the street, just missing the paperboy. He lobs a newspaper onto the steps, in return. Seeing Lady Coulter in the hallway, Margaret calls out, 'Good mornin', Madam,' and thrusts the newspaper into the surprised woman's hand.

Lady Coulter stands rigid and shoots her a cold stare.

Later that evening, Margaret is summoned to the drawing room. Seated on an olive-green chesterfield, Lady Coulter sips her after-dinner port with a detached air. She places the glass on one of the voluted tables, and her attention finally turns to Margaret.

'First, I do not wish familiarity with any of my servants—best out of sight. However, if we are required to communicate, you will address me as My Lady, and when talking of me to another member of staff, you will refer to me as Her Ladyship. Do you understand, Longford?'

'Yes, Madame. I mean, My Lady.' Margaret thinks of Elsie's referential 'that cow upstairs' and suppresses a smirk.

'Second, what on earth has happened to the door knocker, Longford?'

'I am so sorry, My Lady. I do not know what you mean.' Margaret racks her brains. It was there this morning.

'Well, the previous gal got it glittering like gold on a summer's day. It's not up to standard.' Margaret's face flushes, and seeing her point has hit home, Her Ladyship speaks softer. 'Please try harder.'

'Yes, My Lady.' Margaret grits her teeth and resists the temptation to curtsy.

'And another thing, Longford. If you need to give me something, it must be on a silver salver.'

Margaret remembers playing on Brighton beach with her brothers as a child, and the gentry calling away their children before they got too close. She leaves the drawing room feeling small and unappreciated. And dirty.

Margaret lies on her bed, staring at the ceiling. With no windows, the attic room is hot and airless, and she struggles to breathe, as if someone dumped a sack of King Edward's on her chest. Her body aches like never before, and her hands are red-raw. She longs to pack her bags, but her mam has enough on her plate. She can't go home.

Fortunately, she gets on well with the other servants, those who deem to speak, that is. As kitchen maid, she is the lowest of the low, and there is a strict pecking order. She even serves the other servants their meals.

'It's good practice,' Elsie says, grinning.

Margaret likes Elsie. She comes from the countryside and knows life in the raw. She's down to earth and doesn't flinch when emptying the gentry's slops, or groan when lugging hot buckets of water up three flights of stairs so they can have a bath. Gladys keeps herself to herself. Pretty with long blonde hair, she's vacuous in a way men seem to like. A secret admirer sends her silk stockings, trinkets, and chocolates.

After dinner, they have a giggle, watching legs pass by the high window: men's legs in baggy trousers. One-inch turn-ups swaying above tan and white shoes, or black boots, round-toed and chunky. The occasional linen spats, off-white with pearl buttons.

'Ooh, swanky,' Elsie says.

And women's legs in black silk stockings, peeking beneath long hems of sleek straight skirts and silk crepe dresses—some hems two inches above bony ankles; some even higher, revealing fleshy thighs and suspenders.

'Ooh, I wouldn't dare,' Elsie says.

Then they share their magazines—*Pegs Paper* and *The Red Circle*—filled with romantic stories about wealthy, handsome heroes, sweeping poor young women off their feet.

Margaret also reads books, which she borrows from the library. On her afternoon off, she snuggles up in the attic room with her latest: Agatha Christie's *The Mysterious Affair at Styles*.

Not to be outdone, Elsie produces a little book of her own: *Daily Prayers for Servants*, a Christmas gift from Her Ladyship.

Margaret Skims through and reads a paragraph out loud: '*Almighty Father, make me feel that in Thy providence Thou orderest all things for the best, and grant that I may be satisfied with the station in which Thou has placed me, not envying those who are richer and higher than I, but content to be poor and lowly in the world.*' There's more, but she stops, with a snort. 'Oh, my Gawd. I'm so happy, having the privilege of making their bleedin' lives so sweet and comfortable.' She flings the book across the room and returns to her murder mystery, immersing herself in the ruminations of Hercule Poirot's little grey cells.

Gladys is sick every morning. Margaret supposes she is coming down with the flu, but when her waistband noticeably expands, Elsie comes right out and says it.

'Are you expectin', Gladys?'

Gladys won't tell who the father is. The gentry won't keep her on with a baby as it reflects badly on them and, and with no family for support, she may end up in the workhouse. So, Margaret and Elsie help her try to get rid of it. They buy bottles of pills: pennyroyals, Beecham's, and quinine; give her hot mustard baths; make her shift heavy armchairs around the drawing-room; and, on her day off, they get her jumping on and off benches in the park. But someone must have informed Her

Ladyship because, next thing, Gladys packs her bags, and is never seen again. At least they gave her a month's wages, which they didn't have to.

Margaret and Elsie exchange glances, and Elsie lifts her eyes upstairs. They suspect who the father is, and he's not a million miles away from Her Ladyship's shiny brass doorstep.

Margaret has no intention of ending up like Gladys. But when you have two half-days off a week and one full day off a fortnight, it's difficult having a relationship with a man, never mind meeting one in the first place. In addition, with five girls to every man, the competition might make a girl do something she hadn't ought.

On Sunday afternoons, she and Elsie take a stroll in Hyde Park. The soldiers look so handsome in their uniforms with their scarlet jackets.

'Don't tell them you're a skivvy,' Elsie says. 'They'll run a mile.'

'Well, they've no cause to be so high and mighty,' Margaret says, indignant because many soldiers were cottage boys before and had little choice but to join the army. Nevertheless, she wears gloves, hiding her red hands.

A month ago, she met a young man at the Sunday dance in the church hall, and he asked her out. But he wouldn't dip his hands in his pocket to buy her a bag of chips, which put her off as it didn't bode well for married life. Another young man she walked out with was plain ugly. Hoping he had other redeeming qualities, she tried to engage him in conversation about books, mentioning authors such as Conrad, Henty and O'Henly, who write boys' stories. But the young man's gormless expression showed he didn't have a clue what she was talking about.

Margaret believes marriage is the way out of domestic service, and, since she doesn't have much else going, she adheres to the mantra that the way to a man's heart is through his stomach. So, she starts paying more attention to Cook, who really does turn out some exquisite dishes: delicious and a picture to behold. Margaret hadn't noticed before.

The amount of food the gentry put away amazes her. They have the best quality food delivered daily: a man brings milk, cream and eggs, and another brings fish, flapping in a bucket of seawater, fresh from the beach. Much food arrives from Fortnum and Masons, packed in attractive wicker baskets. Even breakfast is a veritable feast for the gentry: bacon and egg, sausage, finnan haddock or kedgeree. Margaret compares it to the plain food they give the servants: herring, cod, stews and milk pudding; and to her poor parents, who eat toast for breakfast, and how her mam buys groceries on tick. She remarks to Cook about the unfairness of it all: the gentry don't work, while hard-working folk are starving.

But Cook has none of it. 'Know your place, girl! Think yourself lucky and give thanks for what you do 'ave.' As an employee of her Ladyship for more than 20 years, Cook's loyalty lies with the family.

Margaret says nothing more, realising she is barking up the wrong tree. However, she has heard whispers of discontent from servants of other houses about shorter hours and better working conditions, like the factory workers won.

Miss Susan, Lady Coulter's daughter, breezes into the kitchen, wearing a loose, knee-skimming lilac dress with a 60-inch-long pearl necklace swinging across her flat chest. Short, chin-length hair frames her delicate features—accentuated with bright red lipstick, blusher, and thick black mascara. She wreaks of cigarette smoke and walks past Margaret without seeing her.

'Dear Mrs Ilford, friends from Italy are coming to stay,' she gushes. 'May we use your lovely kitchen, so they can make us some real Italian cuisine?'

'Of course, Miss Susan.' Cook clasps her hands in genuine delight. 'And don't you worry about making a mess; I'll have the maid clean up after.'

Margaret is kind-hearted, but she can't help feeling a stab of envy in the pit of her stomach: of similar age, Miss Susan has all life offers, without lifting a finger.

The following morning, Margaret hands in her notice. Plenty of other positions out there—she fancies being a cook: better pay, and the other servants and the gentry treat you with more respect. 'An excellent cook is worth her weight in gold,' Cook always says. Margaret thinks she has picked up enough to get by in her own kitchen, not that Cook has taken the trouble to teach her anything. Possessive of her recipes, she likes to think the way she makes everything so tasty is a big secret. 'Ha, that's my special recipe,' Cook always says, tapping the side of her nose. But Margaret buys a copy of Mrs Beaton's cookbook, just in case.

Cook is furious when she finds out Margaret intends to leave: the ceramic bowl's contents spill over and drip down the side, like molten gold. 'Ungrateful child. Servants nowadays, you teach them all you know, and off they go.' But there is nothing she can do.

Her Ladyship is another matter; despite her criticisms, she doesn't want to lose Margaret; hard-working, trustful servants are scarce. Margaret braces for another interview. She has learnt it best to adopt a passive, expressionless demeanour and remain silent when dealing with the gentry, even though you are a tumult of resentment underneath. That way, you show them deference and let them get the last word in. Besides, she relies on Her Ladyship to reference her next position. Her Ladyship requires careful handling.

Margaret assures her that she has been happy in her employment and is hugely grateful for learning her craft in such a prestigious household— what a blessed opportunity! However, a position has arisen nearer home. 'And they pay more,' she adds, with a delicate cough.

That's the clincher because no way will Her Ladyship pay Margaret more money, as the other servants will expect a pay rise too. 'Oh, well, I'm sure we will have no problem finding a replacement, Longford,' her Ladyship says, with that air of indifference. And with a flick of the wrist, she lets Margaret go.

Margaret leaves the drawing room and sighs with relief. She cannot wait to get out of the bleedin' place, truth be told.

Penance

Martha fishes for the slither of carbolic soap and grabs a white collar off the side of the stone sink. Working up a lather, she scrubs a stubborn, heart-shaped blemish, then, settling into the task, she steals a glance at the figure beside her: cropped fair hair, flushed left cheek, scabby cut above the eyebrow; shorter than herself and thinner, perhaps. Hard to tell beneath the oversized brown tunic they make them wear. Hard to tell if the figure is male or female. But no men are allowed in this house of fallen women. A bead of sweat trickles down the slender nose, clings briefly to the tip, then relinquishes to the abyss beneath, conjoining with its elemental kind.

'Have you come from the mother and baby home?' The figure whimpers like a soul in torment. And again, louder, 'Have you come from the mother and baby home?'

Talking is forbidden in the laundry. Silence is a general rule, Martha was warned. But the woman becomes more agitated and, fearing a scene, Martha replies through clenched teeth. 'No!'

A black-veiled nun materialises out of the steam, flicking a thin strip of leather like a serpent testing the air.

'I am so sorry, Mother.' The woman falls to her knees. 'Please forgive me. I won't do it again.'

'Pray to God for forgiveness, Mara,' the nun says. 'Another word, and you will explain to Sister Stephen why you cannot keep your mouth shut.'

Martha keeps her head down and concentrates on scrubbing, until a sharp stab in the kidneys makes her wince and she looks round. The nun hovers like an overbearing conscience and points the offending cane towards a giant iron press in the centre of the room, indicating she wants Martha to help fold the oversized items.

Martha complies and grips two corners of an enormous rectangular white linen sheet, knees buckling under the unexpected weight. Mara grasps the opposite ends, and they step back and forth in a kind of dance macabre—*Forward to the middle and back to the bar.*

The movement reminds Martha of her sixteenth-birthday celebrations in the church hall. Music and dancing. Her stepfather insisted on the final reel. He held her tight, so tight she inhaled his whiskey breath and gasped for air. He whirled her round and round till she stumbled and tripped and clung to him for fear of falling. After that, he started sniffing around, giving her the eye.

The folded sheet gets smaller, and the two women get closer. Martha looks Mara in the face for the first time: full red lips, narrow gap between her two front teeth, green eyes flitting like a caged sparrow. Thirteen or fourteen? She looks no older than a child. A blighted rose, never to bloom. Their eyes meet, and Mara looks down. Next time, Martha holds her gaze: intense, unflinching, and they make a connection. Allies in Hades. They place the folded sheet in a large basket with the rest and wheel it to the back door, ready for collection the following day.

That night, Martha searches for Mara's shorn head amongst the rows of beds. She soon finds the familiar profile and whispers in the exposed ear.

'Hello, Mara.' Martha touches the girl's bare arm, and she blinks to consciousness, like a dazed fawn. 'It's alright. I won't hurt you. What were you talking about in the laundry?'

'Have you seen my baby? Have you seen him?' Eyes wide open now, Mara grips Martha's hand.

'No. Shush. I don't know what you're talking about. I don't know what I'm doing in this hellhole. Me mam brought me here to the Sisters of Mercy. Best out of the way, she said, and that the nuns will train me for a job.'

'The nuns took my baby,' Mara says, her voice cracking. 'I was still nursing him. They chopped off all me hair and changed me name. Said I was nobody, and nobodies can't mother a baby.'

'But where's the baby's father?'

'He was so handsome and kind; bought me chocolates and silk stockings. I was a maid in a big house, and when I fell pregnant, they sent me here. For me own good, they said. I must pay for mortal sin and pray for forgiveness, or I'll go to hell. Me proper name's Gladys. It's Gladys, not Mara.'

'Feck's sake don't start her off again,' an aggravated voice croaks from the next bed. 'This *is* hell, girl. Get bloody used to it.'

A key rattles in the dormitory door, and Martha scurries back to her own bed. She pulls a blanket over the side of her face, keeping one eye on the door. Two nuns drag in a limp, half-conscious woman and dump her on a vacant bed.

'Let that be a lesson to you,' one nun says. 'There's nowhere to run. Nobody wants the likes of you. Settle down and pray to God for forgiveness.'

The nuns lock the door behind them, leaving the woman sobbing in the dark.

Every Sunday, the inmates of Sisters of Mercy walk a mile to the village church. A brief reprieve from the claustrophobic laundry, the fresh air cools their scalded skin, and they blink like moles in the sunlight. They walk in pairs in an orderly line, with two nuns flanking each side as a precaution against runners. Some villagers, whose game is to gawp and heckle the weekly parade of sinners, hang around doorsteps and lean against trees on street corners. Respectable young women giggle and blush, while young men shout lewd comments:

'Is it true you get your knickers off for anyone?'

'Bet your gagging for it, cooped up in that laundry.'

'Dirty whores!'

Some hurl stones and clods of earth, as well as abuse. The nuns look ahead, believing humiliation is part and parcel of the women's penance, and if a missile hits the target, all the better. The older villagers stay inside, the shame unbearable if one of their own walked past.

The penitents sit in two pews, especially reserved, at the back of the church. The priest mounts the altar, and mass begins. *Our father, who art in heaven.* In holy chorus, the congregation joins in. *Hallowed be thy name, Thy kingdom come, Thy will be done on earth as in heaven.* The Lord's Prayer reverberates around the church, through the open windows, out into the village and beyond.

Martha wonders if she laundered the priest's vestments. His immaculate white surplus envelopes his torso like angel's wings, making a significant contrast with his underlying black cassock: *nullus modus vivendi.* A spotless collar tops it all off, like icing on the cake. Behind the altar, sun streams through the Crucifixion, and light dances on the altar, bathing the priest in a rainbow of colours. *For thine is the kingdom, the power, and the glory, now and forever, Amen.* Women sob in the dirt at Christ's feet: Mary, the virgin mother and Mary Magdalene, the repentant prostitute. And Martha thinks how lucky men are, made in God's image, and how unfair it all is: women are the ones who suffer.

After Mass, Mara hangs back, wanting to ask the priest about her baby: a man of God will surely have compassion for a mother and child. She dips her forefinger in a small decorative font of Holy Water screwed to the wall, crosses herself and kneels in a pew, awaiting her turn. In her head, she lists her transgressions since her last confession: late for dinner; spoke in the laundry; imagined Sister Stephen's head forced through the mangle, then squashed in the iron-press, brains splayed like the mush she feeds them. But she had better keep that one to herself.

Her turn, at last. She draws-back the scarlet curtain of the confessional box and perches on a stool facing a wooden grill. Making the sign of the cross, she whispers to the priest's black silhouette:

'Forgive me, Father, for I have sinned,' and she recites her misdemeanours.

'God bless you, child.' The priest gives her penance of five Hail Marys.

'Thank you, Father.' She makes the sign of the cross for a second time but falters before leaving. 'There is something else, Father.'

'What is it, child?' His heavy breathing rasps through the grill.

'It's my baby—I just want—I want to know he's alright, Father.'

'Come here, child.'

Thinking he has information; Mara walks round to the other side of the confessional. She parts the curtain an inch and peers inside. Seated on an elaborate carved throne-like chair, cassock pulled-up over his knees, the priest's right-hand jolts up and down, intent on resurrecting his flaccid purple member.

'Yes, come here, child. I want to help you,' he breathes.

She knows what he wants, but he is a priest, and she feels sick at heart. God the Father, Jesus the Lamb and the blessed Holy Spirit drop out of the sky, and she turns away in horror and disgust. He will deny everything, of course; it's all her fault, somehow. So, she keeps quiet and doesn't tell a soul.

'Slave labour. Same thing day in, day out. I'm not learning a damn thing. I want me wages.' Martha demands payment for her hard work in the laundry.

The lines on Sister Steven's grey face crease into furrows of mock humour.

Martha demands to be released. They are keeping her here against her will. She is a prisoner.

Sister Stephen nods her head, understanding Martha's frustration. But her mother placed her in the sisters' care. Martha is young and pretty, best kept out of temptation's way. Another unwanted mouth to feed would only burden herself and the community. Hard work and self-denial, like the Sisters practise, are the ways to happiness. It is best for everyone. The Sisters merely carry out God's will, providing for poor and unwanted women of the world: women like Martha. Sister Stephen sincerely hopes Martha is not ungrateful and will not be a problem. She rests her hand on her belt, feels the tip of her cane, and sighs.

The two young women whisper under Mara's blanket in the dormitory. 'We can't get over the wall,' Mara says. 'There's glass cemented into the top. One girl got her hands shredded. She dropped to the ground, and the nuns thrashed the living daylights out of her for trying it.'

'Once you're here, you stay,' the voice from the next bed says. 'That bitch in the laundry was one of us. She took the vows last year. Fifty years, she's been here. Fifty years!'

'Why don't you come with us?' Martha asks, afraid the old woman will report them.

'They will find and bring you back, and it will be worse.' The old woman has worked in the laundry for a long time, herself. Lost track of the years. With them not celebrating birthdays, she's lost track of her age. She once dreamed about getting out, settling down and living a normal life. But no one came for her, and she had nowhere to go. It's too late, now. Besides, she wouldn't get far, virtually crippled with arthritis and her varicose veins a constant torment. 'I won't tell them. Good luck.' She closes her eyes and turns to the wall.

'We must get well clear of the laundry,' Mara whispers. 'If anyone in the village sees us, they'll turn us in.'

'We could go to my aunt's down in Cornwall. She never did like my stepdad.' Martha recalls her aunt's kind face and the way she complained about 'the dirty bastard' her mother had brought home.

Despite the old woman's forebodings, the pair plan their escape well into the night.

Each morning at seven, the van arrives to collect the baskets of washed and pressed laundry, which it then delivers to churches, hotels, and various locations throughout the district. The nuns have cornered the market in that respect. With a guaranteed steady supply of employees: desperate women, prostitutes, orphans, and unmarried mothers, who they can exploit without paying wages, the nuns offer low rates to local businesses.

This morning, O'Leary, the van driver, is in a hurry; his brother is getting married today, with a knees-up celebration in the church hall after. Lucky to have snared such a canny lass, with so many sniffing around, everyone says. So, when the nun unlocks the back door, O'Leary has no time for idle chatter.

'Good morning, sister,' he snaps and hurls the baskets into the van, not noticing the extra weight.

Two miles down the road, with a skid, he pulls up outside an inn on the edge of town—his first drop. Eager to finish his round early, he flings open the van's rear doors and grabs the basket without looking. Two scarecrow girls leap out, pushing him over.

'Christ Almighty!' O'Leary lies on the ground, unsure what to do. He doesn't want any trouble, not this morning. Nervous, he checks the other baskets. Dishevelled laundry spills out, but nothing's touched the ground, so no mucky sheets to explain.

He stares into the distance, shakes his head and chuckles; then, whistling a merry jig, he continues business at hand, as if nothing had happened.

Already specks on the horizon, Martha and Mara run for their lives over the fields, holding hands, screaming like banshees.

Nine days

D^{ay One}

Roadblocks. Cars bumper to bumper. Drivers shouting, exasperated. No red buses trudging along, bursting with people. No black taxis playing dodgems, weaving in and out of traffic. Ellen finds a parking space two streets down and heads for TUC headquarters. She ascends the narrow staircase, knocks on the office door—out of politeness, rather than formality—and strides in, throwing her hat on a chair. Placing her briefcase on the desk, she waits, hands on hips, poised for action.

Gerald Barlow stands at the window, surveying the chaos below. A strong, well-built Lancashire man, brown hair greying at the temples, he's done a fair share of hard work in his time. Accustomed to the whirlwind that is Ellen Wilkinson, he turns, drawing on a pipe.

'Glad you could make it.' He reaches for a comradely handshake. 'The reaction to the strike call was immediate and overwhelming. We were expecting it, but it came at such brief notice. Transport, gas, electric, printing, iron, and chemical works joined the miners: around two million workers downed tools at midnight. It's bloody marvellous. We need to dispatch you to the North as soon as possible.'

'Of course, I'm glad to help. I'm thrilled, in fact.' Ellen nods her head, eager for instructions. 'Something needs doing; the poverty is heart-breaking. I see it in my own constituency.'

'We want you to visit the coal mining communities and rally support: a show of solidarity from our union representative. Let them know they are not alone, that there's an army behind them. You're the best man for the job, Ellen, so to speak.'

Dedicated and hardworking, willing to storm any platform, she knows the North like the back of her hand. She lodged in the workers' homes on her tours of the mining villages and steel towns: respectable men and women, working too hard, crowded together in cramped houses.

'A reporter from *Plebs*, the socialist newspaper, will accompany you, Frank Taylor. An easy-going, friendly sort, he will observe and take notes. Make use of him.'

'Glad of support.' Ellen scribbles in her notebook, as Barlow fills her in with details: names, addresses and phone numbers—useful contacts. Then, placing her notes in her briefcase, she stomps out of the office.

Ellen lodges with Felicity Adams at her flat in the West End whenever in London. Fifty-something, Felicity is wealthy, unmarried, and a well-respected benefactor of the Arts: literature, theatre, anything that takes her fancy. She first met Ellen on a literary evening and immediately liked the political, fiery young woman.

'My dear, you look exhausted.' She fusses over Ellen, delighted to have the pleasure of her company again. 'I will tell Janet to run a hot bath, then she can cook us a lovely meal. But what about this awful strike? Lady Aldridge is mortified because she can't have her delivery from Harrods. Shall we all starve?'

Ellen fills her in with what she knows: reductions in the miners' wages, increases in their working hours and the appalling conditions their families live in. 'People won't listen, and the government is apathetic.'

'Well, I'm glad we British aren't like those excitable Russians,' Felicity says, perplexed.

'The TUC wants a peaceful strike, with no demonstrations and no rioting,' Ellen reassures her. 'It's a withdrawal of essential services to illustrate the workers' value.'

'They say the mines aren't making enough money, but I've had good returns on my shares this year. I've not given a thought about where it comes from.' Felicity's little luxuries and frivolous spending seem trivial now. 'Let me know if I can help.'

'You're very kind.' Ellen pats her hand. 'I wish others like you were more sympathetic.'

Warm and glowing from a hot bath, Ellen snuggles into a pink dressing gown and sinks into Felicity's deep sofa. Janet, the maid, brings her a fluffy omelette and a mug of decadent hot chocolate, and Ellen relaxes, her concerns melting away in a rare moment of pleasure.

Day Two

'You are too thin, my dear. You should look after yourself.' Felicity insists on breakfast.

'Satisfied, Mummy?' Ellen scoffs a smoked kipper and a glass of orange juice.

'You will thank me later when you can't get a decent meal in those filthy coalfields. By the way, Mrs Carmichael rang from Edinburgh. She went for a golfing weekend, and now the trains aren't running, she's stranded. Such inconvenience.'

'Oh, the poor dear,' Ellen says, sarcastically. She manoeuvres towards the front door, overnight bag slung over her shoulder, briefcase in hand. Frank Taylor is picking her up at seven, sharp. 'Bless you, Felicity,' she says over her shoulder. 'I'll be in touch. Take care. Bye.'

Frank waits on the pavement outside: slim, handsome, clean-shaven, with pale blue eyes. He looks the reporter type in his beige trench coat and loosely fastened tie. 'Miss Wilkinson, I presume?' He smiles and removes his trilby, revealing short slicked-back light brown hair.

'Call me Ellen; we may be together for quite a while.' She grins, looking for his car.

'I parked in the next street. Wait here, won't be a jiffy.'

A boy on a bicycle thrusts a newspaper into Ellen's hand, just as Frank's car pulls up.

Frank jumps out and opens the boot, grabbing her bag.

'I can manage.' Ellen flings it in herself.

Frank settles into the driving seat, and their journey begins.

'The papers are striking, too, aren't they?' she says, holding up the newspaper. 'What's this then, *The British Gazette*?'

'I've heard of it,' Frank says, 'Edited by Churchill. Full of government propaganda.'

'Baldwin is on the front page.' She skims through the article. 'He has proclaimed a state of emergency. Says the General Strike is a challenge to Parliament and the road to anarchy.'

'Playing it like that, are they? Making the strikers look like anarchists and commies, getting the public onside.' Frank takes his eyes off the road for a second and gives her a sidelong glance. He has heard of her, of course. With her shock of red hair and colourful clothes, she made a stir when she arrived in the House of Commons as MP for Middlesbrough East: the only female Labour representative. Her immortal words, 'I am not a lady. I am a member of Parliament.' hit the headlines. A staunch socialist, once a member of the Communist Party, but she distanced herself when the Labour Party proscribed communists. She is smaller than he expected and frail-looking, but she exudes energy like an electric charge. Five feet of dynamite.

Leaving the city behind, they travel northwards. The Pennines, dotted with sheep and spring lambs, roll by, giving way to the black chimneys of the chemical works and the red glow of the ironworks. They drive on, past the river Don and out into the coalfields.

'We've a fair distance to cover: Doncaster, Banbury, Stockton and Darlington.' Ellen consults her itinerary. 'However, the Yorkshire Trades Club is our first port of call.'

The secretary's wife, Beverly Armstrong, is there to greet them.

'We're the lucky ones,' she says, launching straight into pressing matters of the desperate coal mining community. 'We earn three pounds a week, and I've paid a shilling a week into a clothing club for eight months in case the strike lasts a long time. Some folks claim dole, but most struggle with no income whatsoever.'

'Right, tomorrow, I want to visit a few locals.' Ellen takes charge. 'Have a chat with the families. See how they're coping.'

'Some folks don't mind visitors, and I take them a bit of food,' Mrs Armstrong says, relieved at Ellen's arrival and her willingness to get involved.

Although things are tight, she has prepared supper for her prestigious guests: a good old Yorkshire brew and homemade tea loaf. Ellen and Frank tuck in, chatting like old friends, and Frank thinks he wouldn't wish to be with anyone else on his northern expedition.

Day Three

Despite being well into spring, the morning is chilly and drizzling with rain. In the distance, the pit-gear looms over smokeless chimney pots, and slag heaps writhe with women and children searching for bits of coal to sell.

Ellen and Frank meet Mrs Armstrong on the main road on the outskirts of the village, and they walk down the narrow street together. Peppered with coal dust, all the front doors look the same. Mrs Armstrong taps on the third one down and pushes it ajar.

'It's me, Mrs Stubbs,' she says, almost whispering. 'I've brought some bread and a lady from the union, Miss Wilkinson, has come all the way from London to see us.'

'Come in,' a weak voice replies.

A table with two chairs and a filthy rug comprises the furnishings of a cold square room. At the far end, a young woman lies on a bed, covered in a blanket speckled with coal dust.

'Bill's out, searching for coal,' she says. 'The bairn's just dropped off.'

'How is the little one?' Mrs Armstrong approaches the bed.

'Not good, grizzlin' all night.' She pulls back the blanket, revealing a mucky, twisted sheet.

'May I see?' Ellen peers into the bed. Squeaking rather than breathing, the baby looks like a wizened old man, naked and undernourished. 'Don't you worry, Mrs Stubbs.' She lays a comforting hand on the young woman's arm. 'We will help you and the baby.'

'Oh, thank you, Miss.' The young woman's eyes fill with tears.

Mrs Armstrong leaves half a loaf of bread on the table on their way out.

In the house next door, an elderly couple sit swathed in shawls in front of an empty grate.

'An ounce of tea and sugar for you, Mrs Weaver. Don't tell anyone, or they'll be jealous.' Mrs Armstrong winks at the old woman. 'This is Miss Wilkinson, from the union.'

Ellen takes Mr Weaver's hand, cold and bony, like he's in the grave already.

'My Henry worked down the pit for sixty years, man and boy,' Mrs Weaver croaks. 'And look what he gets for it: dry bread and water, and no coal to keep ussens warm. When the strike ends, he won't have a job, and he'll lose his pension.' She wipes her eyes with a filthy rag.

Henry grunts in affirmation, shaking his head at his wife's sordid account of his life.

Ellen bends, so her eyes meet his. 'You are courageous, Mr Weaver. We are here to help. Stay strong. You are not alone.'

Back at the Trades Club, Frank, pale and drawn, runs his hand over his five o'clock shadow. 'It's inhumane. Conditions are appalling. I didn't realise. Can't they apply for poor relief from the local authority?'

'Problem is the pit is open. If the men refuse to work, they are not destitute, and the poor law Guardians have no power to relieve them.' Ellen is wise to the tricks of the pit-owners, having witnessed acute poverty in her own constituency.

'Then the pit-owners have got them over a barrel. They will starve the men back to work.'

'Exactly.' Ellen writes in her notebook. 'I'm staying here another day; things are desperate. That baby needs nourishment and warm clothes, or he won't be with us much longer.' She sends Frank to town to telegraph Felicity, requesting immediate monetary assistance, knowing she will love to help, if only to ease her own conscience.

Day Four

Ellen sets about organising a women's relief committee made up of volunteers from the village. The pit women are on the front line, and she wants to hear their views. Most are glad to be involved, besides it gives them something else to think about.

Suggestions come thick and fast:

'Make sure everyone has a decent meal every day, especially the kiddies. Some folks don't like charity, but we must care for everyone.'

'We could set up a canteen, where we bring food and share it out.'

'What about clothes and shoes? Some kids run about in bare feet. I'm happy to pass on what doesn't fit our lad anymore, to them what's needy.'

'Well, I'm worried sick about my husband, Arthur. He mopes about all day and hardly says a word, then bites me head off when he does. Doesn't enter his head to help me with the housework.'

Ellen understands. Coal mining is a man's job, and the coalfields observe a strict division of labour. But since the strike, a role reversal has happened where women do the work while men sit at home and do nothing. Many men feel emasculated and depressed, and Ellen's presence, a *female* trade union representative, is not helping matters. Perhaps she can arrange for AJ Cook, the General Secretary of the Miners' Federation, to visit the village. That would boost the men's morale.

'Ladies, thank you,' she says, addressing the pit-women. 'You have some marvellous ideas. We will put together a plan of action regarding soup kitchens, clothing and food parcel distribution and set up appeals for funds. Remember, we are in this together.'

On her way out, Ellen overhears a pit-woman say to her friend, 'She's one of us, ain't she,' and feels very proud.

That evening, Ellen settles down to compile a report about her observations and recommendations.

Frank, just back from town, bursts in, waving a newspaper. 'Behold *The British Worker*, the TUC's answer to *The British Gazette*.' He quotes: '"We are not making war on the people. We are anxious that ordinary members of the public shall not be penalised for the unpatriotic conduct of the miners and the Government."'

'It looks rather thin,' Ellen says, frowning.

'Only four pages. Churchill requisitioned the bulk of paper supplies. But at least we can get our messages further afield and combat the Government's vile propaganda.' Frank sits and watches while she writes. 'Barlow says you've to move on to the next town and speak to the miners there, a show of solidarity and all that.' He notices how she keeps flicking her mop of red hair out of her eyes and feels a rush of tenderness. She is unlike any woman he has known, unpretentious and self-confident. Probably not eaten since yesterday. He would dearly like to take care of her.

Feeling his eyes on her, she looks up and smiles, her cheeks colouring.

Day Five

They make an early start, leaving Mrs Armstrong in control of the relief committee.

'I wish you could stay longer, Ellen,' she says. 'The women look up to you. You've shown them someone important cares. You've given them hope.'

'I have faith in you, Edna.' Ellen leans out of the car window. 'You can do this. The women depend on you. I'll be in touch.'

And they drive off in a cloud of coal dust.

Through the smoky air of the church hall Ellen recognises several familiar faces from the Labour Movement. They raise a hand and nod in her direction, and Ellen waves back. These are her people.

She hands her hat and coat to Frank and takes her place on the platform. Her face flushed from the heat, wearing her characteristic red frock, she stands before the angry crowd like a living flag of revolt.

They hang on her every word, cheer with her passion and shake their heads in sadness with her compassion. After an hour, her voice shakes with tiredness, but with her heart and soul, she flings a final message of defiance:

'We must put the miners first. If the Government and pit-owners defeat them, we are enslaved!'

Cheers shake the building. Frank catches Ellen as she descends the platform and places a protective arm around her waist.

Later, he whisks her off to a restaurant in town. Seated in a candle-lit corner, he takes her hand and reveals his feelings about how she has opened his eyes to the dreadful inequalities, and about how he can't bear to part from her when the strike is over.

'I've enjoyed being with you, too, Frank.' Ellen's head still reels from the thunderous reception at the church hall, and the fizzy wine blurs her vision. 'We do make a splendid pair, don't we? I am fond of you, but I am dedicated to my work, you know.'

'Yes, I know, and I respect that. Could we be together, though? Might you consider marriage, perhaps?'

She smiles at his coyness and squeezes his hand. Her eyes shine, and he leans over and kisses her softly on the lips. She reciprocates and is for a moment lost. But she draws back.

'We've much on our plates as it is. It'll keep, won't it, Frank?'

'Yes, my dear. It'll keep. Let's talk again, after the strike.'

Thinking of her strict schedule, she whips out her notebook and checks plans for tomorrow.

Day Six

London looks different. Tanks and armoured cars rumble up and down major roads.

'Christ, it's like there's a war on,' Frank says.

'There is—a class war,' Ellen replies. 'The Government set up a distribution centre in Hyde Park, after an incident at the docks. Barlow told me on the phone. They use tanks to break through the picket line and escort lorries safely into the city.'

'But who's driving the buses?'

'Volunteers recruited from the public and students from Oxford and Cambridge. They think it's all a bit of a lark. The Government prepared for the strike, apparently. Well, they've had nine months while the Samuel report was going on.'

The traffic crawls, and six strikers march past, waving banners.

'Workers of the World Unite!' They chant in unison. 'Not a penny off the pay, not a minute on the day!'

Frank pulls up behind a stationary bus and stretches his neck out of the window. 'The strikers are blocking the road.'

'Blacklegging bastard!'—an angry yell, followed by the smash of broken glass.

'Crikey, a striker's thrown his banner through the bus's windscreen. Now he's punching the driver,' Frank reports to Ellen.

'Stop that. Stay where you are, I say.' A policeman runs across the road, brandishing a truncheon.

'Good Lord, it's Henry. Lady Aldridge's butler.' Ellen recognises the policeman. 'I bet he volunteered as a special constable. He will never catch them.'

Henry's helmet tumbles to the ground, revealing his bald head, and the strikers scuttle off, hurling obscenities.

The traffic moves, and Ellen focusses on her current mission.

'Right, first things first. Let's see how Felicity is getting on with the fundraiser arrangements.'

Barlow has arranged for Ellen to speak at a fundraising dinner: a posh affair with prestigious guests. She knows some of them from the literary circle, and some are friends of Felicity—her donations to the miners' cause are already most generous. An opportunity to gain substantial subscriptions, but the dinner party will require tact and persuasion to convince the upper-class guests to support the miners.

'Good to see you both,' Felicity gushes. 'One worries, with the tanks and such frightening news on the wireless. Strikers overturned "The Flying Scotsman" in Newcastle. Is there a revolution, after all?'

'It won't come to that,' Ellen says. 'It's different here; we must go through the constitution. Tensions are running high. It's understandable. There are a few outbreaks of aggression, but no one is plotting a revolution.' She turns the conversation round to the dinner party. 'How are preparations going?'

'Fabulous,' Felicity says. 'I've hired the theatre, not much else happening there, and have sent out invitations. Some well-connected people are coming. I have their word on it. We begin with a delicious three-course champagne dinner, then, when everyone's full and merry, you give one of your wonderful speeches, and we get lots of money for the poor miners.'

'You are a marvel, Felicity. A first-class organiser, yourself.'

'I presume you are staying overnight, my dear?' she says, spotting Ellen's bags.

'Of course, if you'll have me.'

Frank books a room in a hotel, and before leaving, he slips a kiss onto Ellen's cheek, which she doesn't mind at all.

After he's left, Ellen settles down on the sofa, sipping a glass of sherry, intent on completing her latest report. But shattered from the events of the previous three days, she falls into a deep sleep.

'Good night, my dear. Sleep tight', Felicity whispers. She covers Ellen with a blanket and switches off the light.

Day Seven

'Can I tempt you with a buttered croissant and some freshly brewed coffee?' Felicity asks, greeting Frank the following morning.

'I've eaten breakfast at the hotel, thank you,' he replies.

Ellen bursts in with a flurry of papers and a sense of emergency. 'I'm meeting Barlow this morning at headquarters. Hand in my reports and catch up on developments. Frank, you stay here and help with last-minute preparations for the dinner party. Are we having music, Felicity?'

'Oh yes, four chaps from the literary society formed a little jazz band. No cost. So good of them.'

'Your irresistible charm may have something to do with it.' Ellen picks up her briefcase. 'Right, see you both later.'

Frank spends most of the morning on the telephone, confirming bookings and negotiating prices. At last, he replaces the receiver with a satisfying click. 'I wrangled a dozen cases of free wine. The chap's grandad was a miner, and he wishes us all the best.' He beams at Felicity.

'Ellen will be pleased. How are you two getting on? Must be difficult living in someone's pocket you barely know. And in such circumstances.' She had noticed the goodnight kiss.

'You're very attached to her, aren't you, Felicity?' he says, surprised by her cold tone.

'She is a diamond. An absolute diamond. Capable of great things. Have you seen how she can move a crowd? I would hate anything to come between her and her work, her destiny.'

'You think I'm a threat to her career as a politician? You were a suffragette once, weren't you, Felicity? Went to prison for the cause? Haven't you women got what you wanted?'

'But so many other challenges face women now that we have the vote, and the professions are open.'

'Do you expect Ellen to sacrifice her happiness for the greater good?'

'Ellen's duty is her happiness and her fulfilment.'

'What about marriage and family life? What about love?'

'Marriage takes so much more out of women.'

'Well, we will have to let Ellen decide for herself, won't we.' Annoyed at Felicity's interference, Frank worries she'll influence Ellen against him. But Ellen has a mind of her own, and she did say she is fond of him.

At that moment, Ellen sweeps in, and an awkward silence follows.

'Everything alright, comrades?' She would hate anything amiss between her two favourite people. 'How are preparations going?'

'Everything is fine, my dear', Felicity says, not wanting a bad atmosphere. 'Frank has secured a bargain on the wine, so it's all ship-shape and Bristol fashion.'

'Splendid.' Ellen's tone turns sombre. 'Some strikers have returned to work, and the Government is protecting them. Not the miners, though.' She holds up *The British Gazette*. 'According to the latest edition, the transport situation has massively improved. Thanks to the volunteers and strike-breakers, two hundred buses are on the road. But Barlow says it's all lies to undermine the strikers. Oh, and the bishop says it's a sin against God to strike.' She throws the newspaper in the bin.

'Unbelievable.' Frank snorts. 'Will they stop at nothing?'

'They perceive the strike as a challenge to the constitution, and they cannot let the unions win. Both sides are desperate to reach an agreement. For the sake of the miners' families, we must stick by them to the end.'

Day Eight

Ellen is not out of place amongst the well-heeled of the West End of London; a Member of Parliament for six years, she has debated the middle-classes in the House of Commons and socialised with them at the obligatory social functions. She is, however, a million miles away from the slums of Manchester, where she was born and brought up, and where her father toiled in the cotton mills. She owes her strong work ethic to him. A staunch Methodist, he believed an individuals' destiny lies in their own hands: it is up to them to avoid poverty through hard work. 'I pulled myself out of the gutter,' he said. 'Why can't others?'

But education and experience have taught Ellen that the system is loaded against the lower classes. Poverty is not an accident, a temporary difficulty, a personal fault: poverty is the permanent state in which capitalism forces most citizens to live. Many of those in whose company she finds herself this evening: socialites, shareholders, and the wealthy have not done a day's hard work in their entire lives.

Dinner party well underway, bellies full and appetites satisfied, gentlemen light up cigars and ladies admire each other's jewellery.

Ellen takes the stage.

All goes well to start with. She describes the starving babies and the old folks shivering by empty grates; and the upper-class audience feels sorry for the mining communities. Then, appealing to their intellects, Ellen tries to make them understand what the strike is about.

'The miners just want a decent living wage. What can you do if nobody listens? If your family is hungry?'

But then the questions.

A young woman stands, self-conscious, unused to speaking in public. 'It is most unfortunate,' she giggles, egged on by a friend. 'But they have been striking for just eight days; how can they be starving, already?'

'The miners' pay has gradually decreased over two years, and for eight months, they've worked short-time hours,' Ellen says. 'That's what people don't realise. They lived in abject poverty before now, and the pit owners want to further cut their wages.'

A be-whiskered, overweight gentleman stands. 'Ah, but I know a pit owner who pays his miners four pounds a week. Plenty to feed a family on. Pure greed if you ask me.'

'That is a different system, where teams of miners share their pay. It works out not as you think.' Ellen is familiar with the system and knows the gentleman is mistaken.

He returns to his seat with a disapproving grunt.

'But why should we help feed them?' Another lady asks. 'They are like enemies, holding us to ransom. We can't go about our daily business. They are ruining our lives.'

'Damn Bolshies!' The overweight gentleman stands, again. 'They will ruin this country. Starving? Nonsense. No one need starve, too many doles and pensions.'

The hackles on Ellen's neck rise; all she sees are fur coats and sparkling diamonds. Her anger and bitterness spill out: 'Your comforts and luxuries depend on the underpaid work of the miners!'

Titters and gasps from the audience. They don't understand. They don't want to understand. Not seeing the ugly truth ensures the reproduction of their class privileges.

Ellen reins in her anger. 'Please, give what you can. It is most appreciated. Thank you all for coming.' She stomps off stage, afraid of what she might say next, and leaves the theatre, knowing where her loyalties lie.

Day Nine

Ellen speaks to Barlow on the telephone, all morning. Felicity hovers in the background, trying to make sense of the one-way conversation; judging by Ellen's distressed tone, it doesn't sound promising. Pale and teary-eyed, she finally replaces the receiver.

'Whatever is the matter, my dear?' Felicity asks.

'The TUC has called off the strike.' Ellen's voice breaks.

'Goodness, so soon?'

'Unconditional surrender. Something about legalities. It's all been for nothing. The miners are worse off than ever. Barlow is devastated. I can't believe it.'

For once, Felicity doesn't know what to say; nothing is appropriate.

'Whatever is that noise?' She looks out of the window. People walk past the flat, waving Union Jacks, blowing party horns, singing a hearty rendition of 'Rule Britannia'. 'Oh dear, some people are happy about the news.'

'It's alright for them. They will never know what it's like to be poor and hungry. I'm going back up north.' Ellen packs her bags, refusing Felicity's offer of scrambled eggs. 'I can't eat now. I feel sick to the core. You are an angel, Felicity, thank you.'

'But what about Frank?'

'If he calls, tell him ... tell him, I'm sorry.' She wipes away her tears. 'The miners are still striking. I can't let them starve. My constituents need me more than ever. I must go.'

Felicity gives a triumphant smirk. Frank had better find another woman to care for; destined for greatness, Ellen will forge a path for other women.

Equal Pay for a Working Day

'They've feckin' fobbed us off again,' Effin' Eileen says, not one to mince words.

'That sort of talk won't get us anywhere.' Lil, the shop steward, tries to keep the peace, but she's fuming too. Every year, the machinists put in a plea to Ford Management, with the same result: ignored or side-lined with excuses. 'It's a diabolical liberty.' Lil is just warming up. 'We are skilled workers, skilled machinists, yet we are on the same grade as janitors that sweep the floor. And men on nights, doing the same job as us, get paid 15% more. It ain't bloody fair.'

'And we must pass tests on three different machines to get a job in the first place. So why shouldn't they recognise us as skilled?' Sheila says: another machinist and Lil's confidant.

'It's just the way it is, ladies, sorry.' Bernard, the trade union convenor had brought the machinists news of their regrading at Grade B: unskilled. He is reluctant to press the issue. Irrespective of the skills involved, women are paid less than men: men are the breadwinners. Even the union sees more value in men's work; it's common practice.

'But it's not right, Bernard. It's sexual discrimination.' Lil won't drop the matter. 'You must do something. Get off your bleeding arse and help us.'

'If you were men, I'd say you've got to protest. Fight. Show them you mean it.'

'Strike, you mean, don't you, Bernard? We must strike.' Lil stands on a chair and addresses the women sitting at their sewing machines. 'Right, you heard what the man said, ladies. Let's have a proper democratic vote.'

Pamela sits amongst the machinists. She has worked at Ford's for two years, grateful for the boost to her housekeeping money. She hasn't given her pay a second thought, but now Lil says it's not fair men are paid more for doing the same job. A few bob extra in her wage packet wouldn't go amiss.

The women have a show of hands, and Pamela raises hers. Not all of them vote in favour, but it is unanimous.

'Right, that's it. Everybody out!' Lil roars with a sweep of her right arm. 'And we ain't coming back till we get what's right.'

Pamela grabs her flask, coat and handbag and joins the other women.

''Ere, where are you lot off to?' The male supervisor watches in disbelief as they head for the exit.

'We are going home,' Lil says.

And they do, all 187 of them. No machinists mean no seats. And no seats mean no cars. Production at the Ford assembly plant grinds to a halt.

'Come on, love. It's time I was gone.' Pamela taps her freshly polished nails on the bedroom door.

The pips on the radio announce seven o'clock, and Tony Blackburn chuckles, 'It's going to be another hot one.'

On the settee, two kids read *Korky the Kat* and eat *Lucky Charms* out of blue and white striped cereal bowls Pamela swapped for Green Shield Stamps. Smaller portions than usual, so the box lasts longer. At least she knows they *are* eating; grumbles of free school dinner soggy chips, cardboard corned beef and wallpaper paste rice pudding worry her.

Besides, they live off chips at home: chips and beans, chip sarnies, chips and the occasional sausage—when the hardship fund runs to it. Potatoes and lard, she has plenty of.

The radio blares, '*It's alright I'm jumpin' Jack Flash; it's a gas gas gas,*' and Mick emerges from the bedroom. Tufts of curly brown hair poke through his string vest, and his belly sags over pyjamas bottoms held up with frayed cord. He stretches and yawns, which turns into a wolf-whistle when he spots his wife dressed up in her glad rags.

'How's me little Revlon babe this mornin'?' he says.

Pamela is wearing her best frock: the flowery blue cotton one she bought from Kays catalogue for parents' evening—paid off, thankfully. And to accentuate her still-pretty features, a bit of red lippy, mascara and baby blue eyeshadow because Mick said it brings out her eye colour.

'Well, the press might turn up, again. Want to look my best.' Pamela smooths her shoulder-length brunette hair in the mirror, and Mick puts his arm around her waist, squeezing her tight. 'Don't love; it took me ages to iron this frock.' She kisses his cheek and pushes him away with a giggle. She picks up the Tesco carrier bag containing the banners she was up half the night making and hovers by the front door, casting an affectionate eye over her family. 'Be good for your dad, kids. See you later.'

'Don't fret, love. We'll hold the fort.' Mick joins the kids on the settee, and they squeal in protest as his fingers fish their cereal bowls for fluffy bits of sweetness.

Pamela throws a kiss and leaves the flat. Over the balcony, she spots the red top of the no 7, winding through Dagenham town centre. The lift had better work, difficult running down ten flights of stairs in your heels.

'Oi, you lot back at work yet?' A tight home-perm pokes out of door 116. 'They've laid-off my Ernie, thanks to you lot. No food in the cupboards and bills need paying.' A baby squeals in the background.

'She should be home, looking after her family,' the woman's husband shouts from inside. 'Selfish cows should be ashamed of themselves.'

'I am so sorry, Vera. But we have no choice.' Pamela and her neighbour were friends up until the strike. She truly regrets the hardship the dispute is causing. 'It won't go on for much longer, hopefully.' Pamela breezes past, not wanting another argument.

The bus driver spots her wobbling down the street in his mirror and waits a minute. He picks her up every morning. Same time. Same place. Regular as clockwork.

'Mornin' comrade.' He grins, as she gets on the bus. 'Bit overdressed for the picket line?'

'We're canvassing around Whitehall today.' Pamela feels important. 'Want to look smart, don't we?'

Creating the right impression is essential, the strikers had decided. 'We don't want folks thinking we're slovenly slags out for a lark,' Sheila said. 'We are respectable married women, and our wages go towards the welfare of our families.' She gave a sidelong glance at Mandy in her mini-skirt and plunging neckline and sniffed. 'Well, most of us are.'

The bus driver looks Pamela up and down. 'Proper glamour puss, you are. I'll keep an eye on the newspaper. Pin you up at the depot. The lads will love it.' Not in the mood for harmless flirting, she ignores him and makes her way down the packed bus. He turns round and shakes his clenched fist in a gesture of support. 'Hey, give the money-grabbing bastards what for, gal.'

She smiles back in appreciation. An elderly man offers his seat, but she politely declines, sensing he needs it more. But he insists, so she sits with a grateful sigh and watches the rush hour traffic through the window: men and women commuting to work—factories, shops, offices, who knows where.

The bus stops at a red light, and a blue Ford Anglia pulls up beside in the outside lane. Pamela's dad used to have one just like it: day trips to Southend-on-Sea; family packed in like sardines; the wind messing up her hair; a fly stuck in her throat, making her choke; and her mam shouting, 'wind that bloody window up.'

The lights turn green and a brand-new Ford Escort—bright red with a sporty spoiler—nips in front of the Anglia. Mick fits the door panels at the assembly plant. He keeps talking about buying one, but they have enough on the never-never as it is. Besides, they are saving for a coloured telly. She casts a discerning eye over the Escort seat covers: black with a red flash just off-centre and red piping around the edges. They look fantastic; could be her machining. It requires a particular talent, fitting together the bits of material the management dumps by the sewing machines, working out which piece goes where, lining up the seams and sewing them together with exquisite, neat stitching. Sheila said the machinists ought to stitch their initials in the corner, like artists do in paintings.

Pamela spots the gigantic neon italics of the Ford logo and gathers her bags. The river Thames is eerily peaceful, and the sky, under normal circumstances blemished with white fumes pumping out from six tall silver chimneys, is clear blue today. Ford management had no alternative but to close substantial portions of the assembly plant with 9,000 workers laid off, and 40,000 more jobs at risk.

On the tarmac outside the closed steel gates, stands a crowd of fifty-five women: a conglomerate of beehives, perms, handbags, cardis, faux pearl necklaces, Crimplene two-piece suits, flowery cotton dresses, mini-skirts, and long dangling earrings. Fag smoke curls busily skywards. Women in their thirties, mostly. Like Pamela, they've had their babies and gone back to work. The job gives them some independence, and they have fun, despite working in an old shack with an asbestos roof that lets in the rain and is home to mice and rats. In winter, the women's breath is visible and the management wheels-in portable electric heaters. In summer, they sweat cobs, and the management sends round lime juice and salt tablets.

A hand in the crowd waves Pamela over. 'How's Mick coping?' Eileen asks, taking a drag on a Park Drive.

'He's good as gold.' Pamela refuses a cigarette. 'Trying to give up, ta. Yeah, kids have never seen him so much. He does a bit of dusting and hoovering to help, even wears my pinny, and he's a dab hand at beans on toast.'

'Do him good, a bit of women's work. I wish my Ernie were more supportive.' Eileen blows a smoke ring through pouting lips. 'Down the pub, every feckin' chance, boozing away the hardship money. He says we're taking the mickey, putting them out of work for the sake of a few quid extra.'

'He'll change his tune when you bring in a wage packet to match his own.'

'Not sure about that. Think Ernie would rather have me chained to the kitchen sink.'

'I've never been on strike before. I'm scared but excited.' Amidst high-pitched chatter and nervous laughter, wide-eyed, Pamela surveys her fellow strikers.

The coach pulls up, and the women pile on. They canvassed the city, marched through Hyde Park and Regent's Park, last week. But today is special: the strike leaders have an appointment with Barbara Castle, the Secretary of State for Employment. She wants to help resolve the dispute.

After an hour and twenty minutes, the coach arrives in Westminster. Lil takes Sheila, plus two others, and they head over to the Houses of Parliament. Pamela and the rest search for a strategic spot to stage their protest. Settling on a grassed area by the busy main road, they position their homemade banners and placards. Pamela was saving the big box the new fridge was packed in, in case they couldn't keep up repayments, but it's the perfect size. She also sacrificed her best cotton bed sheets: cut them into long strips and attached a stick to each end. She borrowed the kids' felt-tip-pens for writing slogans in her best handwriting:

SUPPORT THE DAGENHAM FORD MACHINISTS

and

EQUAL RIGHTS IN PAY AND GRADING

Before long, the women attract the attention of passing motorists: some wave and sound their horns, and some even shout over:

'I'm off at six. See you later, darlin'.'

'Oi, here's my phone number, love.'

Pamela waves back, thrilled by the response. 'Didn't expect we'd get so much interest. Nice, though.'

'Working-class solidarity, that is,' Eileen says. Then she screams, pointing to her banner. 'Oh, my Lord, look what it says.'

WE WANT SEX

'You ain't unrolled it properly', Pamela giggles. Eileen unfurls the entire banner, so it reads:

WE WANT SEX EQUALITY

'Bloody 'ell. No wonder they are interested.' The women laugh for a good five minutes before pulling themselves together to resume the serious matter of the strike.

After lunch, Lil and the others report back from the meeting.

'Mrs Castle is a good un, alright.' Lil beams like she's had the time of her life. 'Straight talking, no-nonsense, and no fobbing us off. She donated a tenner to our hardship fund straight off. And when the press went, she opened the drinks cabinet and gave us all a glass of sherry.' Lil grins in delight.

'We're so glad you enjoyed yourselves, Lil, but what does Mrs Castle think about the strike?' Eileen says.

'Well, she's limited in what she can do, but she will speak with Ford Management.' Lil's expression turns severe at the immensity of the situation. 'I told her we would stay out for a year if need be. But she reckons they are desperate, especially since the Halewood plant came out, as well.'

The strikers just need to stick to their guns, wait and see what sort of deal Mrs Castle can negotiate.

They don't have to wait long. The management wants the women back at work as soon as possible; the dispute is costing Ford millions in exports and is crippling the firm. Barbara Castle successfully negotiates a pay rise of 8% below the male rate with immediate effect, with a 100% rise phased in over two years.

Lil breaks the news to the strikers. They are pleased, of course; their victory means an extra seven pence an hour on their pay. However, the proper fight is for the 'skilled' grade: for them to be recognised as skilled workers, like their male counterparts.

'It's more than just money, though, ain't it?' Pamela says. 'Not every Tom, Dick and Harry can do our job. When Bernard put that pile of material in front of those men, they couldn't even thread the machines.'

'I know,' Lil says, 'and they have promised us a court of inquiry to reconsider our grading. But the issues in this are bigger than us. People are used to women being treated as second-class citizens, so it seems natural we are paid less. But it's wrong. Mrs Castle says it's a civil rights issue, and she's going to push for an Equal Pay Act. But these things don't happen overnight. People must get used to it first.'

Lil takes a deep breath, raises her voice an octave and fist-pumps the air in a victory salute. 'But, for now, ladies, we got the pay rise we deserve!'

Pamela cheers along with the others. Mick will be pleased about the extra money and be glad to return to work. Maybe, he'll start sharing the housework and help look after the kids. She has taken things like that for granted and accepted them, but the strike has shown her how things can change when people stick together. One thing's certain, next time the General Election comes round, she will vote.

Olive's Black Power

South London accent with a hint of singing patois, Olive cusses like a voodoo curse. She clenches her fist, a Caribbean volcano, glares into white eyes, and stabs the cold air with her damning placard:

HANDS OFF US
PIGS

He hesitates, floundering in the unfathomable black eyes, unsure whether the youth is male or female: blue jeans, T-shirt with a black clenched fist pinned close to the heart, shorn afro hair, face alight with arrogance and passion, nostrils flared, as if straining at an invisible leash. He backs off. The demo has been peaceful so far, but things can escalate fast. He doesn't want another riot on his hands. The duty sergeant warned him back at Brixton police station.

Olive was warned too, back at Panther Headquarters—an empty derelict house she and the others had commandeered on Shakespeare

Road. Ferocious energy, powered by utmost belief in the rightness of her cause: the loudest and most passionate of the Panther youth, she is overwhelming. The others will follow, swept along on a tide of anger: a force of nature, like a Saint Catherine's hurricane smashing the imperialist shore. Don't give them an excuse, her leader said. Not that they need one. Skin colour is excuse enough.

But she knows. She's seen with her own eyes, felt the scourge on her own body. The first time, aged seventeen, listening to 'The Israelites' in 'Desmond's Hip City', across the road two policemen dragged a man from his car, kicked his legs from under him and splayed him across the bonnet, like jerk-chicken spatchcock. He stole the car, they said, for how can a black own a Mercedes. Even though he was a Nigerian diplomat in a shirt and tie, even though his wife and child sat inside, watching, terrified, they punched his ribs and half-strangled him till his helpless pleas sounded like a drowning man. Olive and her friend, Liz, ran over, protesting at his rough handling, and onlookers joined in. There was a scuffle, and the police arrested Olive, too. Their racism manifested in bruises and swellings on her arms and face, but their violence hit deeper than that. Perhaps they thought her a man, then. Not that it mattered. She was the wrong colour.

But she knew before that. Age eleven, only one in six black children in the entire school. The white kids stared like they came from another planet—the butt of jokes and taunts:

'Golliwog… Nigger… Get out of our county.'

Tender bodies poked and prodded, like alien specimens, pummelled and whipped with malevolent fists and vicious school ties. Teachers looked the other way, labelled them educationally subnormal: a species behind on the evolutionary scale. So, the black kids cowered in corners, ashamed of their difference, kept their heads down and their mouths shut. But not Olive. She prowled the schoolyard and turned their white gaze back on them, like they were the freaks. Inhuman.

'It coz them don't trust foreigners. Dey tink we want take them jobs and steal them money,' her father said, when she asked why the whites were so cruel. 'Am proud of yuh, no matter wat they say.'

But she knew even before that. Age nine, at the airport, when the chill ripped through her thin canvas coat, and the rain battered like bullets. A river of white faces watched her with hate as she gripped her brother's hand and they ran to the taxi, which took them to their father's house. Welcome to the Motherland.

After the demo, Olive makes her way back to the squat. Along a blighted street with silent rows of condemned and boarded-up houses, windows and doors hanging off hinges where vandals and squatters had forced their way in. On the curb side, two black brothers with braided cornrows peer into the bonnet of a clapped-out Ford Cortina that belongs in the scrap yard. They turn the ignition again and again, but the choked engine sputters and goes nowhere. Young men with no prospects, no qualifications, and no jobs. They raise a hand in Olive's direction, and she waves back with a wide grin.

Past the garish-orange-framed window of the record shop, she slows her stride and nods in rhythm with the joyful calypso beat of 'Jump in the Line'—the sound of summer outrageously incongruous with inner-city mid-winter. Next door, Cedella—a young woman, Olive's age—smiles at her own reflection in the lime green-framed window of the hairdressers, stroking her long black hair she paid to have straightened. She longs to be like the white girls: beautiful.

Mrs Brown hobbles across the road in a threadbare duffle coat, head entombed in a faded purple wrap, exhausted after cleaning the city offices. Later, she will return for the evening shift. But now, several hours spare, she nips home to cook the family dinner. Refugees from civil war and poverty, they fled Ghana ten years ago. She hugs a bag of groceries: mangoes, sweet potatoes, and rice, tight against her chest; a stray mango escapes and rolls into the gutter. Olive picks it up and hands the bruised fruit back with a flash of perfect ivory-coloured teeth.

'Tank yuh, mi dear.' The old woman peers with cloudy eyes that have never seen better days.

Mr Maccy shelters in a hidden doorway, clutching a half-empty bottle. He touches the tip of his crumpled fedora as Olive walks by and straightens the skewed tie hanging around his neck. An intelligent and educated man, they gave him a job on the buses. He couldn't take the disrespect the whites threw at him day after day, so he anaesthetised his misery with rum and gunja and vented his anger on his wife and child.

He came to England for a better life, lured by adverts offering cheap transportation on a ship for those who wanted work and fortunes they could never earn in their own countries. On June 22, 1948, SS Empire Windrush deposited him at Tilbury dock, along with 490 others, including Olive's mother and father: all dressed in their best suits and ties, cotton floral frocks and Sunday hats, their worldly possessions crammed into bulging suitcases. Olive's eyes glisten with pride when she thinks of her courageous mother, sailing into the unknown with her father, leaving her home in Jamaica.

But her tears turn bitter with disappointment when she thinks of their rented house on the run-down estate in Lambeth, mould growing on the walls, sinking with subsidence, segregated from the whites who complain the negro presence devalues their property. Her father, Vincent, operates forklifts in a warehouse; her mother, Doris, assembles radios and televisions on a production line: long hours and low pay just to survive, afraid to complain. A never-ending cycle of hard work, bills, and abuse.

They came from different parts of the Empire: Africa, India, and the Caribbean, full of hope and expectation. But they are all still slaves, poor and downtrodden. They are the same people.

Olive saunters through the open doors of the Women's Centre on Railton Road, inhaling the sweet aroma of hot coffee and spiced ginger cake. Two middle-aged black women gossip next to the counter. Hazel, the receptionist, hums a soulful tune while sorting piles of books into alphabetical order. Her massive frame wobbles like plantain jelly, legs, and arms unrestricted in a flowing cotton skirt and floaty kaftan top with low-scooped neckline, revealing her deep ebony cleavage. Bright green fabric wrapped around her head, held in place by knots tied close to her skull, completely covers her hair. The headscarf is more than a piece of cloth, though: during slavery, white masters forced negro women to wear the dhuku—its traditional name. After that, it became a helmet of courage, signifying resistance to loss of self-definition. Hazel embraces her African heritage.

'Wah gwaan, Olive?' She beams a broad smile and asks Olive if she is volunteering this weekend.

With a self-important smirk, Olive says she will check her diary.

Hazel releases a rich molasses chuckle, but she knows her friend is not joking. Her busy schedule of Panther meetings, office temping work, and A-level study leaves little time for volunteering these days.

Olive settles in a shabby armchair amongst the bookshelves. And, for the first time today, she relaxes, her anger melting away.

Growing up, she spent many hours here: a refuge and an antidote from hostile white society, the women's centre exudes a sense of belonging. In the bookshop, on the ground floor, she read fiction and autobiographies by George Lamming, VS Naipaul, and Samuel Selvon—writers, black immigrants, like herself. And books by African American writers such as Toni Morrison and Maya Angelou. Olive identified with their feelings of anger and desire and gained strength and inspiration from their stories. Upstairs, she attended weekend and after-school programmes organised by the Black Women's Group for the community's children. She received her education here, in a supportive environment, in study groups that discussed and provided reading lists about black history.

Black literature is their way of fighting back: informing and enlightening, breaking shackles of imperial representation and decolonising the mind. They taught her to question authority and to be Black and proud. They also taught her practical skills: typing and shorthand, so she could earn a living. Olive rejects her mother's life, enchained by a large family and trapped in a job she hates. Black people can attain better lives, like the books say.

She skims through *Race Today*—a magazine about Black and Asian struggles worldwide. An article about Indochina describes the peasants' revolt: how they seized back the land from tyrannical oppressors and exploitative landlords and replaced the Government with the People's Republic. Starting with agriculture, they expanded to encompass iron and steel production, and eventually all industry, moving towards a fully socialist society: a society where students and intellectuals are involved in the practical aspects of life, and, in turn, manual workers help develop ideas. This resulted in a community built on co-operation and shared knowledge, benefiting many, not just a few. Olive longs to visit China and learn more about communist ideas.

She is about to leave when Hazel calls her over to reception. Mrs Thomas' son, Devan, has been arrested. He was walking home when the police stopped and searched him—the Sus Law, Section 24, allows them to arrest purely on suspicion: no evidence required. They found a £10 note in his pocket, a birthday gift, and assumed he had mugged an elderly white woman in town. They kicked and punched him till he confessed.

Olive knows the boy. Quiet and sensitive, he's a bookshop regular. She tells Mrs Thomas she doesn't believe Devan could do such a terrible crime and places a comforting hand on her shoulder.

'But them say he done it.' Hopeless tears fall down the woman's face. It's Devan's word against theirs. He's bound to be sent down. Magistrates hate black people, too. The boy will have a criminal record, his future tarnished.

Olive shakes her head and squeezes Mrs Thomas' hand. She knows it's not right.

The front door to the squat is half open. Olive frowns, she keeps it shut. Nothing worth stealing, but last month the owner chucked her and Liz's belongings in the street and changed the locks. She kicked the door in, and she and Liz regained residency. This is their home, for a while longer at least.

Once a laundrette, the building stood empty for years—precious living space, while hundreds of immigrants are homeless. The owner didn't care about it until Olive and Liz moved in. Then he decided he needed it for storage and wanted them out.

Stepping over abandoned washing machine parts, Olive calls her friend's name and climbs the bare wooden staircase. The staircase continues to a third floor: an uninhabited space, with precarious floorboards and no lighting, where no one goes.

Olive alights on the second floor, where the squat is situated. The lower panel of a magnolia-coloured door is cracked, where someone once put their boot through. An A4 sheet of paper is sellotaped to the upper panel, on which Olive has written a legal warning with a black felt-tipped pen:

THIS PROPERTY IS OCCUPIED BY SQUATTERS. WE WILL PROSECUTE IF YOU TRY TO EVICT US.

Olive knows her rights: squatters' rights. The owner must go through the courts to remove them, which is costly and time-consuming. She recalls the frightened face of Mr Andrews, the estate agent, who tried to order them out. He blanched as she reared-up to challenge him, and he half-ran, half-fell, down the stairs.

Grinning, she opens the door and calls out again. But Liz is not home. A multi-coloured rag rug covers part of the floor, sparing their feet from splinters and brightening-up the pastel pink colour scheme. Olive decorated the walls with political posters: a prowling Panther: *You Can Kill the Revolutionary, but You Can't Kill the Revolution*; a negro woman pointing a long spear: *Afro-American Solidarity with Oppressed People of the World*; and a picture of Angela Davis, head held high with untamed afro-hair: *Power and Equality*.

A dark-grey cast-iron fireplace, with tiled inserts depicting spindly lilacs, stands tall and slim against the back wall. The fireplace is a valuable commodity they dare not use; smoke would give them away, and since no one has swept the chimney for decades, they risk being prosecuted for arson. An antique reddish-brown mahogany bookcase with glazed doors, fine astragal bars, and adjustable shelves was in situ when they moved in. Olive uses it to store her A-level books: Hobbes', *Leviathan*; Lenin's, *State and Revolution*; Marx's, *The Communist Manifesto*; as well as a stash of magazines: *Black Dimension, Freedom News* and *Race*.

She drops a Typhoo tea bag into a mug, fills a kettle from a bottle of water and plugs it in a socket above the skirting board. A Panther friend had shorted the electric supply, so at least they have light and heat. Rolling a cigarette, she sits on a mattress on the floor and settles down to study. She shivers and leans over to switch on a portable three-barred electric fire. Next to it, Liz's latest read, *If They Come in the Morning*, is spread out on the floor like a gunned-down doctor bird. Strange, Liz is so careful with her books. An upturned mug of lukewarm tea, and a length of cigarette ash in the jam jar lid they use as an ashtray, suggests she left in a hurry.

The thud of boots, stomping up the stairs, shakes the floorboards. Olive spills her tea and grabs her bag, ready for a quick exit. Half-a-dozen policemen burst in, like a neo-Nazi army raiding a terrorist hideout: helmets, stab-vests, batons unsheathed.

'Right, you. Down the nick!' It's the policeman from the demo. 'We've got your mate. You can come quietly or not.' He fingers the end of his baton, and the handcuffs on his utility belt rattle.

Olive smirks with a curl of her upper lip. She clenches her fist, holding in her anger. Don't give them an excuse. But they tell lies— possessing a dangerous weapon, no fixed abode, anything to keep her locked up and prevent her returning to the squat. She could handle two, not six. They would beat her and claim she fell, trying to escape. So, she sneers and spreads her arms, as if surrendering, and saunters down the stairs.

She's gone in a flash, out the front door, into the street, and around the back. The rusty drainpipe breaks loose from the crumbling brickwork, as she shins up. She pulls onto the roof, and several tiles cascade to the ground, shattering on concrete below. The police don't follow. She sits and hurls profanity in words she learnt from her father, in a language they don't understand. They wait it out.

The cold air nips her skin, cooling her fiery blood. She shimmies further up the roof and shelters behind the chimney stack, where two grey sky-rats scrap over a crumb. On the horizon, the high-rise flats of Brixton Central rise above the squalor and vanish in fog. Before her, the streets stretch out. Long rows of terraced houses; prominent slanting rooftops of varying heights; clusters of extended chimney pots; bay-fronted multi-paned windows, cracked and opaque with filth; weather blasted mock Tudor cladding; intricate gable ends, whitewashed with bird droppings— Edwardian houses, worn out and in disrepair, leased by extortionate landlords or appropriated by squatters. But once the stylish abodes of wealthy whites, whose fortunes and inheritances derived from who knows where—the slave trade, perhaps.

The pale sun pricks Olive's face. She leans back and closes her eyes, and the late afternoon activities of the neighbourhood wash over her: the mouth-watering aroma of fried onion and saltfish, a radio blaring the bass reggae rhythm of 'Wonderful World, Beautiful People.' The sounds and smells of the Caribbean invade Olive's consciousness, taking her back to another time, another place.

Lazing beneath an evergreen ackee tree, clusters of bright-red fruit nesting above in a splendid architecture of branches; long green grass caresses her skin, as the warm breeze wafts in from the ocean. Red-billed hummingbirds with long, emerald-green streamers whirr in a cloudless vermillion sky; and, in the distance, the hot sun shimmers across flat tin roofs of the tenements.

A screaming siren jolts Olive back to the present. She peers over the roof. The police have gone. How long has she been here, three or four hours? The sky merges between darkness and light. Neither day nor night, but a merging of light and dark. A liminal time.

She scales across the roof, hangs over the edge and kicks through a top window. Reaching down and in, she turns the latch. The saw-edged glass cuts her skin, and momentarily, blood flows like a river; but she stops it with her mouth, like a tender kiss. She climbs through, and there she is on the third floor—till now, an uninhabited place.

Outside, speckled diamonds glitter in the darkness, like the glistening crown of imperialism. But a new dawn is coming; the frost is melting, and new life will emerge, diverse and colourful.

Save Our Pits!

'Scabs Scabs Scabs!'

Miners file through the colliery gates to a crescendo of boos and angry chants.

'Brace yourselves, here they come!'

Angie is caught up in a wave of pickets as they surge forward. They hit a wall of police, preventing them from getting too close, but she's near enough to notice a miner smirk and give his mate a cheeky wink.

'You selfish beggar!' she screams, thinking of the sacrifices her family and others are making.

He turns his head, surprised by the high-pitched voice. 'Look, Scargill's slags! Shouldn't you be at home with the kiddies?'

'Scab!' She spits with pure hatred.

He reaches inside the canvas snap bag hanging on his shoulder, and a ham sandwich comes flying and smacks her in the face.

'Come away, Angie. You'll get hurt.' Sandra, one of her team, tugs her coat, and they push through the barrage of pickets to a safer distance.

Angie takes deep breaths to steady her racing heart and checks her watch. 'Where are the others? Time we headed home.'

At four o'clock this morning, Angie and five other women from their local miners' support group squeezed into her Ford Escort and travelled sixty miles up the M1 to Silver Hill Colliery, Nottingham, for the onset of the day shift. But now Angie must return to her own job as checkout operator at Woolworths; with her husband striking, her family relies on her wages. And some of the other women have kids that need getting ready for school.

Looking around, Angie spots seventeen-year-old Alfie Jones, who lives down her street. He started work at the pit straight out of school. He shouldn't be here; his dad forbade him to go anywhere near the picket lines. The NCB will use any excuse to get rid of miners, and if Alfie is arrested, they will sack him. But here he is in the thick of it, pumping his fists and shouting obscenities.

A policeman grabs his jacket collar and flings him three feet away. Alfie gets to his feet and darts forward; this time the policeman coshes him with his baton.

'Oh my God, Alfie!' Angie, witnessing the violence, runs over.

A solid dark blue uniform blocks her path. 'Get back!' the policeman shouts.

Alfie's on the ground, holding his head in stunned agony. Angie tries to dodge, but the policeman grabs her arms and pulls her wrists together. The cold metal handcuffs pinch her skin and press against her bones, making her cry out in pain.

'Section Four, Public Order.' He reels off the caution and drags her to the riot van.

It's dark outside. The policeman finally lets Angie out of the van, along with half-a-dozen male pickets.

'Bad luck, love,' one mumbles, his mouth caked in blood. He winks a swollen left eye. 'The bastards won't make it easy for you.'

The policeman takes her to an anteroom, with whitewashed walls and bright fluorescent lighting. A twelve-inch-thick stainless-steel door leads to the custody suite at the far end. She sits on a cold bench screwed to the wall and waits her turn.

She hadn't stepped foot in a police station till last week, when a police barricade, just off the motorway on the lookout for flying pickets, pulled them over.

'We're off visiting my old mam, officer. She's poorly with her heart,' she said, crossing her fingers, hoping her lie was unfounded. They believed her but issued her a ticket to produce her driving documents.

Angie's scared but curious; she's seen prisoners booked into the nick on the telly in *The Bill* and her favourite *Juliet Bravo*. So, she knows she's entitled to a telephone call by rights.

'I want to phone me husband,' she blurts. 'He worries.'

'You will have to wait. There's a queue,' the policeman says in a deadpan tone and stares at the wall.

Another riot van pulls up outside, with a skid and crunch of gravel.

'We're full, mate. Go to the city nick,' a gruff voice shouts.

Angie leans against the wall and closes her eyes. It could be a long wait.

At last, a policeman's head appears around the stainless-steel door and nods to the one guarding Angie. He takes her through to the custody suite. Stale urine and disinfectant make her eyes water, but at least it's warmer, here. She glimpses metal bars down a corridor where the cells are, and her stomach lurches as she realises the seriousness of the situation.

Behind a long white counter, the elderly custody sergeant clonks on a computer keyboard. He's retiring next year; thought he'd landed a cushy number but hadn't banked on the miners' strike.

'What have you been up to, then?' He peers over thick, black-framed reading glasses.

Don't tell them anything you don't have to; she recalls from the telly. They can take it down and use it in evidence. She's entitled to a solicitor, but she's not sure if she needs one yet. So, she keeps her mouth shut, except for answering the obligatory questions: name, date of birth, address, ethnicity, next of kin.

The policeman removes her handcuffs, and she empties her pockets: lipstick, hairbrush, hairgrip, half a packet of polo mints, and a phone number scribbled on a torn piece of paper. Then she takes off her shoes and removes her jewellery: Timex watch—cracked in the scuffle, and a silver Saint Christopher, a gift from John, her husband, last Christmas. She tugs at her wedding ring, but it won't budge.

'We'll let you keep that on,' the sergeant says, sealing her belongings in a transparent plastic bag.

The policeman leads her to a small room smelling of Dettol. A female officer takes her fingerprints and mugshots. Angie runs her fingers through her hair, thinking she must look like she's been dragged through a hedge backwards, as her mam used to say.

'Right, get undressed and put your clothes on that chair,' the female officer orders.

Angie stares wide-eyed in disbelief and wonders whether she put clean knickers on this morning.

'It's procedure,' the female officer says, noticing her horrified expression. 'You have nothing I haven't seen before.'

Not wanting the woman's fingers where they are not welcome, Angie complies and whips off her bra and knickers. She raises her arms and straddles her legs, as instructed, turns around and bends over, her face burning. Nothing untoward drops out, so she puts her clothes back on.

The policeman reappears and takes her to a small interview room, containing a desk, a computer, and a portable cassette recorder. He switches the recorder on and cautions her a second time. Then the questions start. What was she doing at Silver Hill colliery? Is she or her husband members of the communist party? Has she ever been to Russia?

Angie thinks she has done nothing wrong, but the way he phrases, rephrases and repeats the questions confuses her, until she believes she has done something terrible and deserves to be locked up.

Silence, while he searches the criminal database.

Since she has no previous offences, she is free to go. But she is on the system now and will be charged next time.

Almost twelve hours since her arrest, relieved the nightmare is over, Angie telephones John to come and pick her up.

'It's a bloody disgrace, putting a woman through all that,' John says. 'Show them the state of your wrists, love.'

Angie holds out her swollen wrists to their neighbours, Beth and Sam. Since the strike began nine months ago, they have taken turns cooking dinner. One week, Angie cooks, and they come round to her house: the next week, vice versa. It saves on bills.

'Mam will have a fit when she finds out.' Angie twists her arms, so they can appreciate the full extent of her injuries. 'She already thinks I'm a disgrace for picketing. A woman should be at home with her family, she reckons. She'd always had dinner on and a plate warming when my dad got home from the pit.'

'Oh, Angie.' Beth examines Angie's bruises. 'You are brave. Can't do picket lines, me. Too rough. I feel so guilty.'

'You do your share, love, helping in the soup kitchen and collecting money for the miners' fund.' Sam pats her hand. 'Besides, you're here for me with a cuppa and a loving shoulder. I couldn't do it without you. In fact, all you women are a bloody godsend.' He neglects to mention he forbade her to picket.

When he was a child, Sam's dad died in a pit accident, making him master of the house and giving him a fierce sense of family responsibility. 'We care about each other in the mining community,' he says. 'We have got each other's backs. When you're down there in the dark, you must be friends, regardless of political or religious differences. You could die down there.'

'Aye, we are all in this together.' John overturns the soggy green mass of cabbage on his plate, searching for meat. Beth had picked a cheap cut of belly pork; white and shiny, it has dissolved in the gravy.

'What about them scabs, though? They're not with us.' Angie thinks of the blackleg and his cheeky wink.

'They think because their pit is profitable, their jobs are safe,' John says. 'But Thatcher wants to shut down *all* the pits. She brought in McGregor to tear the mining industry apart, like he did the steel industry. So, the Nottingham miners are no safer than any of us.'

'How much longer can we hold out, though?' Sam says. 'The Government won't back down like in '74, and Thatcher has tons of coal stockpiled. Some lads are trickling back to work. The Coal Board offering £10,000 redundancy money doesn't help. The younger ones will take it, reckon they can get jobs doing summat else once the pits close.'

'But that's a fantastic amount of money, Sam.' Beth gasps. 'Just think what we could do with it.'

'Nah, think on this, love.' Sam speaks slow and clear. 'After tax, it'll be more like £7,000. And I'll be out of a job and not allowed to claim benefits. That money won't last us long.'

Angie stands to clear the empty plates but comes over dizzy. 'I'll feel better after a good night's rest.' She sits back down.

'Will you be alright for the march tomorrow, duckie?' Beth says. The National Women Against Pit Closures Movement is holding a rally through London, finishing off at a conference centre where delegates from the regional branches will take turns addressing the audience. Her local branch has roped Angie in.

'Course I will. Can't bloody wait.' Angie says, more determined than ever after her ordeal.

Jubilant tones of colliery brass bands reverberate the city air, as thousands of women march out, banners aloft, placards waving.

Unite and Fight. Coal, not Dole. Save our Daddys' Jobs.

A day of solidarity, an opportunity to share stories and garner support: their first time in London, for many. Angie hands out banners as her contingent alights the coach.

'They've just started off. Look, there's Mr Scargill!' She nods towards the familiar figure in brown suit, red tie, and flat cap, chatting to two women. 'That's Anne, his wife. I recognise her from the papers.' She points to a good-looking woman with blonde-streaked brown hair, wearing tailored trousers and a neat black sweater.

'Who's the other woman?' Beth says.

'That's Betty Cook, her friend.' Tall, slim with black permed hair, the woman stands at Anne's side. 'She makes out she's a quiet family lass, loves nothing more than being home looking after her kids. Butter wouldn't melt. But she's been a Labour activist for years. A proper little closet revolutionary. A bit like you, Beth.' Angie giggles and nudges her friend.

'I hope they will both speak at the conference. So inspiring. The strikers think the world of Scargill, don't they? He doesn't ask them to do anything he wouldn't do himself. Even got himself arrested.'

'He's dedicated to the miners, alright. Although John reckons spring was the wrong time to bring them out because folks don't need coal so much. Anyway, he better not lead from the front today. This is our day. Oh, it's alright; he's making his way to the back with the mothers and kiddies. Right, come on then.'

Hoisting their banners, Angie and Beth join the march and break into a chant:

'Save Our Pits_ Save Our Pits_ Save Our Pits!'

They march the length of Downing Street, past no 10, averting their eyes and falling silent out of respect for the two pickets who died early in the strike. Then, fuelled by hatred for the woman who intends to steal their men's jobs and destroy their lives, the chanting resumes:

'We are miners' wives united. We will never be divided!'

The march pauses at the Houses of Parliament, while one of the pit-women hands in a petition to the Queen. Signed by thousands, the petition is accompanied by a letter, beseeching her majesty to step in and assist the miners' cause:

'We have, over recent years, seen the horrors of mass unemployment cripple other industries; we have witnessed the slow death of communities dependent on them and the tragedies that fall on families and individuals.'

Angie and Beth both signed the petition, but some women refused, believing it grovelling to the establishment. Others think Scargill is behind the letter and actually dictated it. But they're all on the same side, at the end of the day: the miners' cause unites them.

The rally organisers emptied the conference centre of chairs and tables beforehand to make more room, but the tremendous audience still overflows into the street.

Betty Heathfield, founder of the Women Against Pit Closures movement, takes to the stage and kicks off proceedings. She thanks everyone for attending and says she's overwhelmed at the dedication so many women have given to the cause.

Next, women delegates from their different regions take turns to talk about their own experiences. Many, not used to public speaking, wobble and giggle, while some read from a script, loud and fierce.

Angie feels sick and trembles. She's comfortable speaking at the Miners Welfare Centre in her hometown: a natural, full of passion, they say. But this is different. Taking a deep breath, she gets on stage. She needn't have worried because the words flow. She tells the thousand-strong audience about her experiences of picketing, about police brutality and about her arrest. She commends the generosity of the other wives, who have selflessly helped the miners and their families. Finally, she explains how the strike is not all about money: it's about their lives, their communities, and their children's futures. Without the pits, the villages will die. They can't let Thatcher win. She finishes to thunderous applause.

Elated and empowered, Angie feels like she has grown wings and can fly.

The announcement when it comes is devastating, though they were half-expecting it.

'We're going back to work.' John swallows his tears. 'Thatcher's won.'

'Oh, love. It's all been for nothing.' Angie says, thinking of the shared meals, central heating cuts and the little pleasures they could no longer afford.

'Don't say that, Angie.' He grasps her hand. 'It's a grand victory for us. A victory for the workers, the way we've come together and fought and never given in. And we've kept it up for an entire year. This country has never known the likes. We should be proud of ourselves.'

'What will you do when the pit closes? At least we have the redundancy money.'

'Plenty of time to think about that. For now, I'm glad my wife's back, and we can return to normal.'

'Well, it might be the end of the strike, John. But it's just the beginning for me.' Angie looks him in the eyes. 'I've learnt about politics and unions and done things I'd never dreamt of. I want to carry on. I want an education. I want to go to college.'

And she's not the only one. Despite the hardship, many women have had the time of their lives. They've organised themselves and enjoyed the camaraderie. They love their families but have no intention of returning to the isolation and the perpetual cycle of cooking and cleaning. Some, like Beth, find contentment in motherhood and family life. But others, like Angie, want more. Need more.

'Well, it's up to you, love.' John sighs. 'Shame to waste your newfound talents.' He hugs her tight. 'My little jailbird.'

She's lucky to have a man like John; not all husbands are so understanding. Some marriages have drifted apart and will end in divorce.

She hugs him in return. They haven't beaten Thatcher, but it has all been worth it somehow. Things will never be the same.

Women's Land

Saturday 21st July, Oak's Farm

Clover stood by my side and wrapped her strong arms across my shoulders, so close I noticed three fine hairs sprouting from a black mole on her neck and how her cheeks dimpled with the effort of concentration. Together, we went through the motions, exaggerating the movements until the dynamics became clear, until the whole became fluid, graceful and near effortless, as if second nature. She whispered instructions in my ear, her breath sweet as wheat, vibrating my ear drum, sending shivers down my spine.

Power comes from the buttocks and thighs; use your arms and shoulders for guiding. Rotate your waist, swinging the blade in an arc from the side, across and in front of your body. Rest on the opposite side, then return. The blade remains on the ground, slices rather than chops, as a sharp knife cuts bread or a tomato. Shift your weight from left to right foot, and shuffle forwards. Create a rhythm, like a pendulum swinging back and forth. Scything does not require great strength. It takes time and patience—a skill to learn.

And I reaped the rewards of her tuition. Two lengths, until I saw her swelling with pride, grinning at my efforts; my knees buckled, and I fell, giggling like a teenager. Eager to share the burden, Hazel and Laurel took turns as well. They managed twenty minutes each till, exhausted, energy spent, they also fell. But their techniques were not good; they swept the scythe upwards, chopping the golden stalks.

Clover worked hardest, as always. The sun hammered down, but she hardly perspired. She made it look easy and cut so the wheat heads all faced the same direction and dropped in neat lines. As she progressed down the field, her shuffling feet left a tramline… swish… swoosh… swish… swoosh… the blade sliced in hypnotic rhythm, while in the distance the roar and crash of the Atlantic collided with the rocky shore.

Born and raised on the weather-ravaged Southwest coast, Clover appreciates more than anyone the value of a good harvest. She tells stories of her family praying for fine weather, of her father paying the village wise woman for spells and incantations to ward evil spirits off the crops—anything for a bountiful harvest. Broad-backed, muscles hard from years of farm labour, she is the strongest of us. Her short golden hair, ruddy complexion, checked shirt and corduroy breeches resemble a man; only when you are near, you realise her gender. When I compare her to my ex-husband, he fails in every way.

As Clover scythed, we followed behind tying the cut stalks into bundles, but not too tight, so air can circulate. Then we stacked the sheaves upright in sixes and scoured the ground for loose grain. The custom is to leave the gleanings—as Clover calls them—for poor people and the birds, but we need food ourselves and the birds are fat enough.

Our yield is double last year's. Aurora is overjoyed, and all credit to her management; she timed the harvest perfectly. Any later and the hard grain would have scattered as we cut the stalks, making our task much harder. And we were fortunate with the weather, which is precarious with sudden vicious storms bringing pelting rain. It was hot, but the gentle coastal breeze made conditions ideal.

Tonight, we feast and celebrate. As I write, Honey, our chef, prepares spit-roasted chicken, while a mouth-watering mixture of home-grown vegetables and wild herbs bubbles in an enormous cauldron. Slabs of warm bread made from freshly ground wheat flour will make a delicious accompaniment, along with a fine selection of home-crafted beer and an assortment of wine: rhubarb, apple, blackberry, and elderflower. Afterwards, Coo, our maestro, will play the fiddle as we sing and dance to old Cornish tunes.

I can't wait to feel Clover's arms around me again. Life is good.

Monday 23rd July, St Erth Secondary School

Dizzy from life, love and happiness, Clover's scent on my skin, I stumbled across the classroom as if half-intoxicated, handing out well-fingered copies of Shakespeare's *Richard II*.

One of my more forward pupils, Jenny Jones, enquired after my health, and I explained how my muscles were sore from the strenuous harvest. She said I was lucky to live on a farm by the sea. And is it true only women live there, and we allow no men?

Aurora warned us against discussing our unconventional lifestyle with outsiders, as they are judgemental. Although I know my students well enough and consider them intelligent and empathetic individuals; their recent essays on our set drama text *The Crucible* were well-written and impressed me. And it is the 1980s, after all. So, I told Jenny Jones we live as a community of sisters, as ourselves [without male oppression].

Like nuns? she said.

Well, sort of, I said. [But we take no vows to God in our community of women-centred living and loving.] I know the villagers gossip, fuelled by curiosity more than anything. But visibility matters to me and seeing me will help others feel brave. So, I came out and said it.

I am a lesbian.

Their inexperienced eyes scoured my body, and the silence was palpable. Unasked questions made the air oppressive and difficult to breathe.

We would never have guessed, Miss, looking at you. Jenny Jones broke the spell with a grin.

It was a joke. But fair comment, I do look mannish these days with no make-up or jewellery, flat pumps instead of high heels, black trousers and a plain cotton shirt, my long dark hair pinned up in a tight bun—I couldn't bear to part with it. Besides, Clover undoes it every night and runs her fingers through, like seagrass.

I turned the class's attention to the text at hand and instructed them to read Act II, Scene I, considering the significance of John of Gaunt's 'This sceptred isle' soliloquy. Meanwhile, on the whiteboard, I wrote, *The Well of Loneliness* and *Oranges Are Not The Only Fruit*—optional extra-curricular reading for those interested. That will get them thinking.

How rewarding today has been. Teaching is not all about facts but about helping pupils realise their potential. I want them to make something of their lives, especially the girls, especially the ones from poorer families who don't have support or encouragement, whose parents think further education and careers are not for the likes of them. Most live in Cambourne, one of the most deprived areas in the country, where indigenous folk struggle to earn a living and pay the rent, while every summer, carefree holiday-makers swarm second homes and holiday lets and invade the beeches.

Aurora has big plans for the farm, hopes one day we will be fully self-sufficient and give up our employed positions. But I love teaching. I have a wealth of experience and want to continue. Of course, I will still hand over my salary every month, as usual. I don't mind; Aurora and the farm have given me so much— safety, hope, a new life. I'm a completely different person now.

Friday 14th August, Saint Erth Library

Jenna Trefethen—another Cornish woman, burned to death. A midwife, healer, and herbalist. Obliterated, blown away like chaff, as if she never existed. I added her to my list—a long list of women tried and sentenced by men: Christian men. Hanged, drowned, pressed to death under heavy rocks. All it took was a whisper, a suspicion, a malicious neighbour with a grudge.

Four years' research. Whenever I insert my disk into the hard drive, the computer whirls like a time machine and takes me back to that fateful day, a lifetime ago. My husband was at the office, Katie, at school. I sipped percolated coffee in the kitchen, as usual, in between hoovering and preparing dinner. The dulcet tones of Radio 2 played in the background— *Romeo and Juliet live in eternity. We can be like they are. Come on, baby, take my hand. Don't fear the reaper.*

A man's voice spoke over the airwaves, authoritative and serious. I listened. He wanted the autobiographies and memoirs of working-class people. Secreted away in attics and cupboards, they are perhaps long forgotten. He is a professor of social history and listeners should send them to him because they are important documents of the past, of how common people once lived. He may include our ancestors' personal stories in the volume he is compiling; their names mentioned, at least. He wanted them.

I recalled Great-Aunt Grace's notebooks, found in the airing cupboard after her death: the musty mothball aroma, the dog-eared corners and faint time-washed title, *Memories of a Suffragette*. And I remembered how she would ramble on about the sacrifices and suffering and chastise me when I couldn't be bothered to vote. Engulfed in my own problems, I never took much notice. I kept the notebooks—a memento mori—though I never read them.

However, after hearing that man on the radio, I did read them. Great-Aunt Grace's handwriting was challenging, but time and patience revealed the horrors of her story: hunger strikes, force-feeding, public humiliation, and police abuse. And I wept because I was so proud of her and never told her. Most of the suffragette's records were destroyed; and, yes, her words were important because they documented a hidden history. But I wouldn't allow some male middle-class professor to appropriate, edit and take credit for them. I swore to publish Great-Aunt Grace's memoirs myself.

The seed was planted. I searched libraries and archives but found little evidence. History is all about men. Where are the women workers, the revolutionaries, and the rebels, like Great-Aunt Grace? What were they doing? How did they feel?

After extensive research, I discovered a handful of texts: poems, novels, and autobiographies. Texts that depicted the lives of women working and living in terrible conditions: workhouses, mills and factories, and in domestic service.

Hard lives. Wasted lives.

And when I moved here to Cornwall, the parish records and local assizes revealed a new era of women's oppression—homeless, desperate women, persecuted, unloved and unwanted: the witches of the Sixteenth and Seventeenth Centuries.

Same old story. Time and time again.

At first, my research was a distraction from my troubled marriage. But my despair turned to anger as I realised my personal problems were the plight of all lower-class women. Their stories strengthened me to find a better life, and I devoured them like nourishment.

We need to see those women who have been overwritten, ignored, and excluded. Erased by a hostile society. I will write them into history— a sister across the abyss of time who knows how it feels to be judged and persecuted. I will tell their stories.

Saturday 15th August, Oak's Farm

A new member has joined our community—a young woman, a lone parent, no more than a child herself: thin and pale, wringing her hands as if she carries the world on her shoulders. Briar brought here, another of her rescue cases. Surviving on DSS benefits, with no family and no support, the health visitor referred the young woman to social services when she noticed cuts on her arms. They appointed Briar her caseworker.

I, too, am one of Briar's rescue cases. I wanted to leave my abusive husband. I wasn't working then; he wouldn't let me. He said a woman belongs in the home, caring for her husband and children. Three million unemployed, leave the jobs for them. Hooked on antidepressants, my self-confidence rock bottom, I became more dependent on him. Then he demanded sex as his conjugal right and beat me when I refused. He wanted to control me, subordinate me. With no money and no place to go with my six-year-old daughter, I contacted Social Services.

I recognised Briar from college years ago, only that wasn't her name then; she used to be a women's libber activist: *burn your bra and pay housewives wages.* She still adhered, judging by her sagging breasts and impudent nipples noticeable through her hand-knitted olive-green jumper. After all these years, she was still beautiful with flawless bronzed skin, shining hazel eyes and cropped black hair. She told me how she and Aurora met and fell in love at the Greenham Common peace camp. After it disbanded, they pooled their resources and rented Oak's farm from Cornwall County Council.

I wasn't a lesbian then, though they let me in. Once my divorce was finalised and the house sold, I would be independent and able to support myself. I could leave Oak's farm whenever I liked; but once here, it felt natural, and when I met Clover, I never wanted to leave. My initial worries about raising Katie in a single-sex community were unfounded. She loves it here as well, and roams free on the land without fear, even after dark.

She is blossoming. Briar says anyone can be a lesbian: it's just a matter of discarding false consciousness of the heterosexual romantic myth.

This afternoon, Aurora summoned a meeting. She said she is not running a refuge, and there are proper centres for vulnerable heterosexual women, but there is nothing for lesbians. We need a haven where we can be ourselves without reprisal. She also prefers new recruits to have a skill or a profession: Coo, a talented musician, is our medical doctor; Honey, a trained chef, studies butchery and tanning at college; Briar, our expert weaver, has already woven multiples of socks, hats, and jumpers ready for winter. Others, like me, help with menial chores and contribute our salaries towards the farm up-keep. Aurora is brilliant and handles the finances and general management. She was an academic before, but there was a scandal. One also must be a lesbian, of course, and there are rules: no men, and we change our names, which we choose ourselves—it must relate to nature: a symbolic casting-off of male privilege and genealogy.

But what will become of the young woman if we turn her away? A few centuries ago, they would have burned her alive. If something bad happened, I could never forgive myself. I voted; she can stay. It was unanimous. We must take care of her.

Monday 23rd August, Saint Erth Secondary School

Mrs Johnson, the full-time English teacher, ignored me. Good morning, I said, and she raced off down the corridor, as if late for the 8:15 from Redruth. She's normally well-mannered and friendly; perhaps she didn't hear me. Then, at lunchtime, she sat with Mr Williamson, the maths teacher, oblivious to my presence. We always sit together and discuss pupils' assignments. I racked my brain, thinking whether I had offended her. But I am too sensitive, perhaps; she has other commitments, after all.

Later, when leaving school, a pupil pushed another girl, so we collided. She yelled, she fancies you, Miss, and they ran away hurling obscenities: lesbo_dirty dyke. I didn't recognise them. Not students of mine.

News travels fast. My nerves jangled, and the old familiar tightness clenched the pit of my stomach. I thought of Clover's soft brown eyes and our warm cabin and headed home.

Saturday 29th August, Oak's Farm

We always touch the massive oak at the farm entrance in passing, for respect and luck—touch wood. But this evening, I stayed for over an hour under the protective canopy of enormous branches, stretching at least sixty-feet tall and outwards, half as broad. I ran my fingers over the extensive nebari that dipped deep into the earth, then resurfaced like ancient, gnarled dolphins coming up for air. Leaning against the vast rough trunk, I willed the tree's strength to permeate my soul by osmosis.

This ancient tree, at least 1000 years old, I wonder what troubles it has witnessed.

In folk tradition, oak trees have healing properties and are home to guardian spirits. Clover collects acorns in Autumn for good luck talisman and charms. She made a necklace for me and placed it around my neck, with a murmur of strange Cornish words I didn't understand.

Last April, while tilling the lower field, we discovered a freshwater pond stone-lined with white quartz. The quartz glows in the moonlight, lending the water a magical quality. Circling the pond, a dozen six-inch holes contained various items: swan skin with feathers intact; eggs containing chicks close to hatching—the shells had dissolved, but the membranes remained; bits of birds—beaks, claws, and tiny skulls; and fragments of cloth in vivid blues, golden yellows, and vibrant greens— 350 years old but preserved in the moist environment. All ritual finds, where hopeful visitors seeking good fortune had deposited scraps. Evidence of pagan worship.

A silver wink above my head, among the branches of the oak, caught my eye. Standing on tiptoes, I grasped a small bundle. Fastened with pins and bound with cotton, it contained heather twigs, herbs, and magpie feathers. Similar bundles dangled from other branches at varying heights, like Christmas ornaments. These were recent additions, though, not ancient offerings like the ones we found before. I removed them. They are dangerous.

I am not a pagan. Brought up in a Catholic household in a small mining community, it seemed natural I married and had children. It was what women did. I never questioned my sexuality. Perhaps I married to escape poverty. Nowadays, I can't think of Catholicism without remembering the atrocities done to women in God's name.

Aurora is tolerant of others' beliefs. She says we must believe in something. A humanist who rejects Christianity and all religions, she says it's all supernatural nonsense, and the Bible is just stories, like any other. George Eliot was a humanist who used a man's name, so people read her books. It must be difficult believing in people's intrinsic goodness when you have suffered discrimination and cruelty all your life. But Aurora says we only get one life, and people are all we have.

I believe in Aurora.

Friday 4th September, Saint Erth Library

Televisions and newspapers are not permitted on the farm. Aurora says they are distractions, and you can't believe what you read and hear. Besides, we are too busy, wrapped up in our own existence to bother with the outside world. But I think it is important not to lose touch; we live on the periphery, but what happens in mainstream society affects us. So once a month, I skim through the newspapers in the library.

I sat at my favourite desk by the window. Outside, yellow leaves from nearby birches rattled on the concrete garden, blackberries shrivelled on brambles and fallen crab apples rotted into mush. Honey would have picked the fruits by now and transformed them into something wonderful. On the desk, a dozen folded leaflets were scattered willy-nilly, as if the distributor had no time to waste. The covers resembled polished black marble slabs, with the letters A.I.D.S. chiselled on the surface.

Don't Die of Ignorance

By the time you read this, 500 people will have died. 50,0000 carry the virus, and the number will rise if we do not take precautions. The virus attacks the body's defences and transmits through sexual intercourse with an infected person. Anyone can get it, man or woman. It can be present in semen and vaginal fluid. It is deadly with no known cure, and it's spreading. If you ignore AIDS, it could be the death of you. So, protect yourself and don't die of ignorance.

I remember when AIDS was first diagnosed. The fear and panic. The problem was nobody knew where it came from and how big it would become. Hospitals were full of dying young gay men, and scientists labelled it a gay-related immune deficiency. At least we know now it's not limited to homosexuals, and you can't catch it from regular social interaction. Many people are still frightened, though; they don't understand. They see homosexuals as plague carriers. The prejudices and discrimination remain.

I thumbed through the newspapers, pausing to read articles of interest.

Breast is Best

Scientific studies show that breast milk contains essential vitamins and minerals and protects against many illnesses and diseases, including respiratory tract infections and acute gastrointestinal illnesses; middle ear, throat and sinus infections; gut infections and intestinal damage linked with a reduction in the incidence of necrotising enterocolitis; sudden infant death syndrome (SIDS); allergic diseases: reduced risk of asthma, atopic dermatitis and eczema. Breast milk is beneficial to the health of your child and is always available. Bottle feeding is unnatural and unhealthy.

And yet, when I gave birth to Katie, scientists were espousing the benefits of bottle feeding. They said artificial foods were as good as breast milk, if not better. Breastfeeding was 'natural' in the past, but times had changed, and people had adapted. Women's libbers celebrated this as a significant step for the emancipation of women from the shackles of child-rearing. No longer would mothers bind themselves to the misery of breastfeeding. They could employ child-minders and find jobs themselves.

Single Parenting Continues to Rise

Over the last eight years, the number of single parents has doubled. 720,000 lone parents are not working and received £1.85 billion in income support. The Government intends to stamp out this culture of dependency. They will phase out single-parent benefits, and help young mothers find work or train them for qualifications. The DHSS will assist mothers' search for absent fathers, enforce DNA tests and make absent fathers pay child maintenance. Scientific studies show that lone parents raise malfunctioning children. Children need a father and a mother figure; how else can they learn their gender roles and function in society?

Imagine having to survive and raise a child on just £55 per week. And now, the government will reduce their benefits and force lone parents into work. My heart goes out to the young single mother who recently joined our community; the worry and immense responsibility must be unbearable. No wonder she was in such a desperate state. I am so glad she is with us now.

Sermon on the Mound

Prime minister Margaret Thatcher addressed Edinburgh's General Assembly of the Church of Scotland. She argued that Christianity is about spiritual redemption, not social reform, and she quoted St Paul saying, if a man will not work, he shall not eat. She also argued that wealth making is good for society as opposed to the redistribution of wealth; the tenth commandment — Thou Shalt Not Covet–recognises that making money and owning things could become selfish activities, but the creation of wealth is not wrong: love of money for its own sake is wrong.

How ludicrous coming from a Prime Minister who has presided over an unprecedented rise in unemployment; closed traditional industries and devastated communities like coal mining, which people depended on for their livelihood. And what about poverty and the growing number of homeless people, will the government let them starve and die on the streets?

But it's all about economics and the vagaries of capitalism, isn't it? This country is experiencing a severe recession, so they want women back in the home, and men off the dole. They demonise single parents and homosexuals who threaten the social order and the traditional heterosexual family structure. Then they appropriate scientific studies and Christian discourse to justify their policies, while displacing their responsibility for supporting the unemployed and the less fortunate members of society.

Thatcher was one of us; she was meant to raise women. Instead, she turned into a handmaiden of patriarchy and capitalism.

Aurora is right; you can't trust anything you read and hear. I am fortunate; I belong in a community where we look after and care for each other.

Saturday 16th September, Oak's Farm

The young woman named herself Cherry. It suits her now her cheeks have a healthy blush. She has a good appetite, too, and relishes Honey's culinary concoctions. We take turns looking after the baby, although I do most. I caught Clover's wistful expression, as I cradled him in my arms—the one thing she can't give me—and quickly reassured her I want no more children.

Although shy and quiet, Cherry has a ready smile for everyone. She wants to earn her keep. Well, there's plenty to do.

Clover and I took her on a tour of the farm, starting in the top field where our South Devon cows graze on lush green grass. Handsome beasts with medium-red curly coats, they are excellent mothers and produce rich milk of 4% fat. Clover promised to teach Cherry how to milk them. They produce excellent marbled beef, too: perfect small farm cattle.

We also own a dozen free-range chickens, a pig, and a flock of Ryeland sheep. Ryelands are a sturdy solid breed with thick woolly coats. Docile and easily handled, content enough to graze near the farm, they don't wander far. Although last May, a tragedy occurred when our flock roamed half a mile away and leaped over a cliff edge. Something must have spooked them because this was so out of character. Since then, we keep our flock penned with a padlocked gate.

We grow crops on the lower field, which is divided into strips. We utilise a four-year crop rotation system_ year one: red clover; year two: potatoes; year three: vegetables; year four: wheat. This method prevents pests and diseases, and the grain requires no fertilisers as it uses the residual fertility from the crop rotation. Besides, a clause in the lease prevents us from using fertilisers or modern machinery: we must use traditional farming methods, which is more challenging. But the land benefits.

On our return, we walked through the meadow, bursting with plants and wildflowers: green-winged orchids; purple primroses; bluebells; three-cornered leeks with long stems and white bell-shaped flowers heads; and pennyworts—large, green, flat and bellybutton shaped. I picked several for Cherry to taste. The three-cornered leek stem is sweet, the flower more pungent. Pennyworts are succulent and excellent thirst quenchers. She will learn to recognise the edible plants. We picked handfuls for a salad, then rested by the stream, brimming with frogs, toads and newts. Dragonflies twirled like mini spinning tops and yellowhammers darted through the copious bracken; overhead, stout buzzards hunted, while gloss-black ravens observed from solid outstretched branches.

Back in the farmyard, the barn brims with our recent harvest. Another week to dry out before threshing and winnowing begins, then we will appreciate Cherry's assistance. We will grind a third of grain into flour with the hand mill, but most we will keep in large wooden vats to last us throughout the year. Last October, a mysterious fire nearly destroyed all our grain and straw stores. We must be more careful, more vigilant.

To end the tour, I showed Cherry the library I am compiling with books written by under-represented women: lesbians, working-class and black women. Books that include positive portrayals and explore identity. I am also organising a storytelling event based around Cornish myths and legends: a re-telling of tales, which displaces men as the leading characters and where women are the protagonists. My idea is based on local legend, Saint Erc—who, in *my* story, is Saint Erca, a woman, who travels from Ireland to free Cornish women from the shackles of patriarchy, the root of all evil. Aurora is my muse.

Monday 19th September, Saint Erth Secondary School

Jenny Jones' father has removed her from school. He is an affiliate of Cornwall District Council.

First thing this morning, the headmaster summoned me to his office. What you do in your own time is your business, he said. But, at school, we have a duty of care to our pupils and must protect them from untoward influences. No more lesbian literature. No more discussing homosexuality in the classroom. He forbids it. Besides, Section 28 of a new Government Act prohibits it. It is against the law.

This was my final warning.

What century are we living in? How would you feel if it was your son or daughter struggling with emotions that society says are wrong, sinful even? How can we help them with advice and counselling if we can't talk about it? And victims of homophobic bullying, how can they ask for help? In my opinion, this Act endangered vulnerable children.

But these homophobic sentiments sounded familiar; they are evident in my research; in the lesbian literature I'd read. Oh, fuck the patriarchy! I am angry and saddened. But I held my tongue by instinct. The school does a great deal for charity, and I know they are kind and caring individuals. I guess their charity ends when it comes to homosexuals.

Tonight, I will hold Clover close.

Saturday 25th September, Oak's Farm

Clover and I hiked across the fields and joined the coast path. A rollercoaster of a walk across high and low ground, along cliffs carved by the sea over millions of years. We made our way down to a shingle beach, where constant landslides on the dark layered cliffs brought down fossils of strange creatures and giant monsters that once inhabited the hidden world of the sea. We rummaged through the shingle and Clover discovered a small spiral-shaped ammonite fossil, perfectly formed, and gave it to me: a symbol of our everlasting love, un-erased by time and tide.

We walked uphill to a copse and carried on through woodland. Emerging from bushes to open ground, the undulating landscape, scarred and crisscrossed with ancient trackways, surrounded us. In the distance, church towers and spires periodically rose through the trees, grabbing our attention. Taking a left fork, we carried on along the coast path and continued upwards towards the summit of Golden Cap.

After a strenuous two-hour climb, legs aching, lungs straining, we reached the top. We sat in silence and watched the ocean—the relentless ebb and flow of waves, like life itself, like human history, endlessly shifting and repeating. As the sun soaked my skin and I inhaled the aromatic sea air, I felt wild and free, and the most relaxed I had felt for months.

We zig-zagged down towards the valley through Saint Gabriel's woods, past Saint Gabriel's house, once a thirteenth century manor house, and by Saint Gabriel's chapel, which smugglers used as a storehouse for contraband. These ruins and a handful of refurbished holiday cottages are all that remains of the mediaeval hamlet.

The sky grew dark as we stumbled back along the coast path towards home; a far-off grumble broke the eerie gloom and on the horizon a flash of lightning struck at the heart of the ocean.

Monday 27th September, Oak's Farm

Reports of strange goings on, Sergeant Kendrick said. Satanic rituals, animal sacrifice, midnight orgies and the like.

I hardly recognised him: his stern expression; the twinkle gone from his unsmiling eyes. He visited us last May, regarding the theft of six hoes and a-dozen spades. He was quite amiable then, swigged Honey's sweet homemade beer, no problem.

Aurora refused to cooperate, of course. He can't possibly believe such nonsense in this day and age. People's imaginations are running amok, or someone is spreading malicious rumours. But what Aurora said didn't matter.

They searched the farmhouse, the outbuildings, and our cabins. They even tipped the mattresses off our beds. What were they looking for? Something incriminating. Anything. They desecrated my library, trampled my books under hard boots and screwed-up my notes like rubbish. Clover was injured protecting my work. A policeman pushed her; she lost balance and hit her head. Blood trickled down her face. Ghastly pale and swaying, momentarily concussed, she resembled some unearthly creature we had conjured up.

Sergeant Kendrick interrogated Cherry. Why is she at the farm? Who brought her here? What does she do all day? Then he took her baby, for his own good. Cherry went berserk, and they took her as well, in handcuffs.

Briar said, once they see her medical record, they will section her and place the baby in foster care.

We are devastated. We must stay strong. We have done nothing wrong.

Wednesday 3rd October, Oak's Farm

Aurora called an emergency meeting. She motioned a long official looking brown envelope in the air, as if spellcasting; then, she slammed it on the table, like a declaration of war. An eviction notice from the Council. We have one month to vacate the farm.

The old familiar dread crept upwards from my belly and grabbed me by the throat. The ground opened, and I was falling, falling. Clover gripped my hand and whispered, It will be okay. We have each other.

I heard others sobbing, as if torn from their mother's breast. Aurora stood firm like the Oak, with Briar by her side. She is determined to fight. She has a contract: five years lease, with three years remaining. A legal document, they cannot break. She will take them to court.

Well, we know about legalities, about how laws can shift and change and be re-interpreted to suit the powerful. They want to break up our little community, and nothing can stop them. One of us could get hurt, and they will forcibly evict us, anyway. We could end up with criminal records.

We must face it; we are no longer safe here.

Friday 31st October, Oak's Farm

Clover carved two wooden rings, and we solemnly pledged our troth beneath the oak, with the tree guardian as witness. She is the love of my life, and I can't envision a future without her. But the true nature of our relationship must remain secret—to the outside world, we are just friends.

I have rented a cottage in Launceston, where I will live alone with my daughter. Clover will find farm work and live close by. We promised to keep in contact with Aurora, Briar, and the others. Nobody knows what the future will bring. One day, we may continue as before. But for now, it is too dangerous. We must go our separate ways.

My studies have taught me that women must write about their lives and inscribe their own history; therefore, I bury my diary at the base of this grand old Oak as testament to how we women once lived, thrived and were happy together without men.

157

–Kelli of Oak's Farm (wife of Clover)

Fill Your Oles Up!

Julie inserts packet lengths of past their sell-by date Fruit Shortcakes into rectangular stationary metal slots, in a training room on the top floor. Kev winks. Middle-aged, tall, and slim, with ginger hair and a military moustache, it's his first day too. His air of authority annoys her, as does the way he keeps looking over, like it's a competition. But he mentions he used to be a prison warden, so she grants him more respect. She does her best, gives out friendly vibes, nods like she's impressed when Kev fills four slots compared to her two, and smiles at the patronising old hand, who demonstrates the correct way to put twelve mouldy biscuits into a machine. 'Biscuit Feeder' is the official job title. But the old hand has done this countless times before and has a £5 bet with the other trainer that they won't last the week. The biscuit factory has a reputation. 'Slave labour' and 'they treat you like shit' are the words on the street.

He passes Julie a light blue cotton jacket with matching elasticated trousers, a floppy, white-peaked mob cap and a hairnet. The mob cap is a challenge. Maintaining an iota of femininity, some women perch it on the back of their heads and fluff out a bit of fringe from under their hairnets; others straggle hair strands down the sides of their faces, like wispy sideburns. Julie pulls the peak down over her forehead and peers out like a nervous meerkat. Jacket and trousers are on the baggy side and smell like Gran's cookie jar, but she approves of the colour, and they're comfortable, like pyjamas. Also, the overall androgynous and homogenous effect appeals: no evidence of breasts, curves, fat bums or skinny frames. It's like one of those Mao suits her O-level Sociology teacher was always talking about.

'Mao suits,' the teacher said. 'We should all wear Mao suits.'

'Wouldn't it be hot, though?' Julie asked. 'And wouldn't the long tails get in the way?' She had mistaken *Mao suits* for *mouse suits*. It was her first brush with communism.

But this factory uniform must be what the teacher meant—this uniform of uniformity.

At the end of a hygienic corridor, the old hand opens a door and heat hits like a blanket. Julie and Kev follow him across a blue metal platform, until they reach a stairwell on the other side. Julie gasps as rising biscuity air sticks to her throat and nostrils and her head swims at the panorama below. This strategic position enables a bird's-eye-view of the vast factory floor, revealing the proficient production of biscuits en masse: six aisles of beige coloured ovens spew out rows and rows of warm biscuits onto conveyor belts; metal arms with slots, like those she practised on, traverse the belts at three-feet intervals and transport the biscuits to wrapping machines, which devour and expel them out the other side in shiny gold and brown packets; blue uniforms place them in large cardboard boxes and take them to the end of the conveyor, where more blue uniforms stack them on pallets ready to be fork-lifted to the warehouse. Each aisle dedicated to the production of one type of biscuit: Ginger Nut, Digestive, Chocolate Digestive, Shortcake, Fruit Shortcake, and Rich Tea.

They safely reach the factory floor, and the old hand points to a brass square clock, with a narrow slit on top, fixed to the wall.

'That's where you clock on.' He speaks louder now, as competition from humming ovens and clickety-clicking machines almost drown him out. Next to the clock, a rack contains many rectangular blue cards, with tiny black numbers printed on the top right-hand side—one for every employee. 'A minute late, and it'll dock you fifteen minutes' pay. Time's money.' He sniffs and takes them to the end of a conveyor belt. 'Chocolate Digestives. You're both on this line.' And with a satisfied nod, he trundles off to find more new recruits.

Kev nudges Julie, and eyes up the chocolate biscuits, licking his lips. She pretends not to see. Kev is a machine-minder. All the machine-minders are men. Julie is a biscuit feeder. All the biscuit feeders are women. She stands beside a machine and glances at her counterpart on the other side of the conveyor belt: blue-uniformed like her, but older, in her fifties, permed grey hair squashed under hairnet and white mob cap. The woman stares into space, chewing.

More difficult now the machine is moving, Julie panics and crams biscuits into slots. They disintegrate like sand before trundling out of reach. Dropping handfuls on the floor, she looks round, worried the supervisor has noticed her adverse effect on profits.

'You'll pick it up, ducky. We all start somewhere,' the woman opposite shouts. Then, disinterested and detached, she continues feeding the machine. Handful after biscuit handful. Ten hours' worth of biscuit handfuls, minus breaks.

'Fill your 'oles up!' White-faced, red-lipsticked and pure evil— 'Elvira' they call her behind her back, although her actual name is Carol. A diminutive five feet and three inches, but the platform shoes put four inches on her height and make her backside stick out, which is counterbalanced by her enormous bust. Like Satan's minion, she patrols the aisle in a maroon-coloured uniform, designating her supervisor status. Waspish black hairs stick out of her hairnet, like crow feathers, and her green eyes glint in the bright fluorescent lighting. A cane or leather sash would suit her, but her tongue prods subordinates into action.

'Whatcha fuckin' playing at?' She elbows Julie out the way, who, besides not filling up her holes, has let four rows of biscuits trundle past. Sweeping up the wayward rows with two hands, Elvira warns, 'You've gorra speed up,' and shoots Julie the evil eye.

Four hours gone. Six remaining. Julie yawns, having difficulty staying awake. The wrapping machine comes to an unscheduled halt. She stretches her aching legs and sighs with relief at the unexpected reprieve. The machine-minder appears, with Kev shadowing, and sticks a long, thin vacuum into the mechanics. How unfair men have monopolised that job; with all the hoovering she does at home, Julie could manage it, no problem.

The wrapping machine stops for several reasons: blockages, when feeders don't fill every slot or when they don't fill slots with enough biscuits—hence, Elvira's manic, 'Fill your 'oles up!' Julie nibbles her fingernails, thinking the halt in productivity is her fault. But further along, another wrapping machine stops, then another. Twenty rows of infinitely recurring biscuits trundle on regardless, heading for the end of the belt, where, if not thwarted, they will drop off the edge, like lemmings. Broken biscuits, sold at a fraction of the price, are unprofitable. Panic ensues.

'TRAY 'EM OFF!' Elvira screams, seeing her bonus going down the swanny.

Mirroring the woman opposite, Julie removes a tin tray from a rack above her head, grabs lengths of biscuits and places them inside in wonky lines.

After several minutes, the machine minders have the wrapping machines working again. The blue uniforms upturn the tins where the belt begins, and the biscuits resume their journey.

An hour later, biscuits come out of the oven half-covered in blotched chocolate. This time the machine minders switch off everything, including the conveyor belt, and production comes to a complete standstill while engineers rectify the problem. Blue uniforms stand dazed, rooted to their spots, unaccustomed to silence and inactivity, unsure what they should say or do now the opportunity arises. The Quality Control manager, Edith, conjures up from behind the oven, looking like a fallen angel with her bright red face and canary yellow uniform. She inspects the biscuits and scribbles notes on a clipboard. Following close behind, Hughie, the engineer, materialises in a thistle-green uniform, like a little Scottish demon. Cursing, feckin this and feckin that, he fiddles with several dials, and consults Edith. Then they both vanish into the factory bowels, till next time.

At two o'clock, the line officially ceases for a thirty-minute dinner break, and blue uniforms trundle upstairs to the canteen. Sizzling bacon and fatty chips clash with the pervasive sweet biscuit smell, and compete for the attention of tastebuds; although, most workers have little appetite, having already gorged on chocolate digestives. Julie is weight-watching and has not yet succumbed to stealing warm biscuits off the belt, but the temptation is strong. She buys a tuna baguette, a bag of plain crisps, and a can of Coke and sits at the end of a long table. The others sit in little cliques, catching up on gossip:

'Michelle's pregnant, again.'

'That Sharon's a lesbian. Lives with her girlfriend and everything.'

'Edith's retiring this year. Won't know what to do with herself.'

They ignore Julie. With a high staff turnover, people come and go, so it's not worth the effort; although Kev seems popular, chatting to three women about the heroisms of prison service. Julie notices the luminescent full moon shining through a high window and thinks how strange, working in this hive of activity when most people are asleep. As a child, she longed for midnight feasts, like the ones in Enid Blyton books, but this is not what she dreamt of.

Besides dinner break, blue uniforms are allowed a couple of five-minute nips when they can go toilet and have a quick smoke, depending on whether production is going well, but mainly on Elvira's mood.

'Go for your nip, Julie,' she hollers from the end of the belt, and Julie nips off before anything goes wrong. They don't have any nips when Elvira's mood is off.

'It's because her husband can't get it up. She's frustrated,' a blue uniform says, causing a ripple of giggles.

A week later, Julie can fill up all her holes, almost with her eyes half-closed, like the woman opposite. And she thinks, this is easy. But the night after, she struggles again; the slots move out of reach before she can fill them. The crafty beggars have sped up the machine, increasing her work output.

Her feet itch, and her legs ache. Ten hours, minus breaks, standing in the same position has adverse blood circulation effects. Most women suffer from varicose veins. Then, she notices a bright red blemish on a Chocolate Digestive.

'Be thankful you ain't on Ginger Nuts', the woman opposite shouts. 'They tear your fingers to bits.'

Julie starts wearing plasters: regulation bright blue ones, quickly spotted if they drop off—imagine the compensation if a consumer found one in a packet. They ease friction, but the insides of her fingers are already red-raw.

A tinny radio, just audible over the incessant humming and clickety-clicking, plays easy listening: 'You used to think it was so easy, but who's crying, who's crying now?' Gerry Rafferty; 'Ooh, I Wanna Dance with Somebody', Whitney Houston; and 'Yes, I do know why I survive', Donna Summer. Sometimes, they put the Indian station on. All bhangra and sitars. Different sounds, different language, same sentiments.

Some women work here all their adult lives. Julie studies their faces and wonders what they think about. Nothing, judging by the blank expressions. Their minds switch off and they go through the motions, like machines. Hands, not heads. Night in, night out. Year in, year out. What does that do to your body? Your brain?

Julie's body revolts. Her mind revolts. Last night, Kev took her for a drink in The Lamb, although she's still not keen on him. He tried it on after. She fought him off. What will become of her, a factory girl? What the hell is she doing here?

The pay's decent—almost £300 a week, more than she ever earnt. Ten-hour shifts. Three nights on and four nights off, then vice versa. The continental shift system, they call it. Plenty of spare time for her real interest and passion in life.

Sweet with the scent of ripe fruits and vegetation, the cool country air cools Julie's hot cheeks. She squints in the bright sunlight, till pale golds, sandy browns, and ruby reds meld into a kaleidoscope of colour. Clicking grasshoppers perform their late summer swan song and humming worker bees gather nectar for the winter months ahead. Julie gently sways in the saddle, the rhythmic clip-clop of hoofbeats soothing her aching limbs and troubled mind. She strokes Robert's soft long neck and runs her sore fingers through his fine mane. The 16.2h gelding, a giant gentleman, is obedient to her requests and never pulls. Over the past several months, his condition has noticeably improved: shining silver-dapple coat, muscles taught and defined, and he gallops over half a mile, without breaking into a sweat.

Two months till hunting season. The farmer is pleased. Julie is allowed to ride Robert out cubbing, with the Quorn next week. And he may let her join the Boxing Day meet in the town centre, as a Christmas treat. What a privilege. He doesn't pay her, but hacking across his land, through the local woods and nature reserve, around the reservoir and monastery grounds—private places she wouldn't otherwise be permitted access—is reward enough.

She steers Robert onto the grass verge, and with a squeeze of her lower legs, he breaks into a canter. A thrill of excitement and a surge of joy runs through her body. The monastery bell chimes ten: time she headed back. She should in bed by noon, re-energising for the night shift. But she has plans. She knows what she wants, and it keeps her going back to that hellhole, for a while longer, at least. She has saved £500 already. She wants to buy a horse.

Still

Heart pumps, blood cruises through blue canals on a journey to nowhere. She can choose not to breathe ... slip deeper into the void ... gulping, like a fish out of water, she gasps stale air. Lungs expand, eyes open.

Dark.

What time is it? She feels for the alarm clock on the bedside table and presses cold plastic against her ear. Nothing. She had gone for a Costa Coffee rather than long-life batteries.

'You get what you pay for,' her old mam always says. Time and money.

She listens hard. Nothing. She tumbles out of bed, stubs her toe on a dead weight, winces and rubs her foots. Dropping to her knees, she feels for scattered fag-ends, in case one's smouldering. In case the whole place goes up, like that Grenfell Tower block on the news. Just because they'd scrimped on money.

Go to the light. Go to the light.

She makes her way to the shaft in the curtains and grabs the frayed edge. No one can see inside her cell in the sky, but she keeps them drawn day and night because she'd seen a horror where a stalker spied on a young woman through binoculars, and she ended up raped and slashed to death. The body lay undiscovered for months until someone complained about the stink to the housing authority, and they found her rotting corpse, all liquid and bone, melding with the limp carpet.

She's not sleeping, and with the electric bill due, she daren't switch on the light.

In the daytime, the view makes her light-headed. Microscopic men mending dirty roads and angry cars jostling on narrow streets. Skipping kids in schoolyards, running willy-nilly, throwing balls, kicking balls, and climbing walls. Self-absorbed lovers in dewy parks and dank alleys, holding hands, kissing, and caressing. All aboard for the sliding, slippery slope of love. Women lug bulging bags, backs bent heading home, dwarfed by gigantic billboards on rush-hour pavements - Lynx, *Africa* body spray: 'Find your magic,' and Britney Spears, *Hidden Fantasy* fragrance mist.

She shivers, breathes on the glass, and sketches her name. A skywriter, far out.

At night, she belongs in the starlit sky. Otherworldly. An unknown entity, aeons away. Part of a special constellation, exiled from Earth for heinous deeds and sent to dwell in outer space. An astral body. She's an alien on a special mission, observing earthlings from a most strategic position. A stranded ET, deteriorating in a hostile environment: translucent skin blemished with redness and pustulous sores, a hacking cough, sleepless nights and days, and pounding headaches. She awaits the mothership. Phone home.

Nothing.

'1,2… 1,2… 1,2,3,' she whispers, testing if she remembers how to speak for when the time comes to communicate. Mam was the last person she'd spoken to. But Mam has her own problems: asthma, her knees, her stepdad.

The week before last, the man at the DSS spoke. She *will* get a job, whether she likes it or not. They won't keep her in idleness much longer, that's for sure. Plenty of work for those who want it. The kid can go to nursery.

She listens hard. Nothing. Dead to the world.

She had hoped for better. She wanted better for her own child. But it's hard. Real hard. She looks out of the window, and a shadowy reflection of her mother stares back.

The spiteful cactus on the sill pricks her hand. Mam bought it for her eighteenth. She came wheezing up ten flights of stairs on June 20th, like a derailed locomotive all out of steam. Forty fags a day and a cleaning job that plays havoc with her varicose veins, catching up.

'Stairway to heaven,' Mam called it. 'All that glitters ain't gold,' she croaked, trying to make her daughter feel better. A mournful dirge. A throwback to Mam's misspent youth. 'Ah, them were the days.'

The lift's not worked for weeks. She counted the steps to focus and take her mind off things. But losing place, she made landmarks.

Step 50 - cobwebby turd and a dry patch of stale piss. Someone didn't make the grade. The smell makes her gag, and she pinches her nose for the next ten steps.

Step 60 - pebble-dash kebab up the wall. Brown streaks and meaty red lumps: an aesthetic contrast with housing authority standard orange, like a modern art piece.

Step 70 - Nazi swastikas and a cock and balls mingle with the legends, 'Paki go home' and 'Boris is a cunt,' craftily drawn by some politically minded artistic type.

'Same old shit,' Mam reminisced.

A long, claustrophobic corridor. Grey plastic floor tiles exude dead horses and sweaty council employees. Then her front door. Regulation dark blue, a square of opaque glass with thin criss-cross black lines and a tiny glass spyhole, which she appreciates more since watching the Horror channel. Same as the rest, except for a glittering 110, marking her place.

She rattles the security chain across and catches her breath, exhausted from the climb.

She eyes the cactus. It *was* lime green with a flower spilling out like hot molten lava on a sunny day, but the blossom dropped off in no time at all, leaving an undernourished shrivelled finger ready to stab her with last-chance sagging spikes.

The kid's goldfish didn't last long, either. Found floating on the surface of green liquid, like mouldy grated carrot. Haunted by distant memories of clear, cool water, flowing streams and glistening horizons, it dreamt of escape, like that pixelated fish, Nemo. But this one lacked comrades, and overcome with sadness and despair, it gave up the ghost on a frosty midwinter morning.

'It's not suited to the altitude,' Mam said. 'Because fish like depth, not height, don't they?' But she'd go the same way, swimming around that bowl all day.

Nothing grows here.

She stifles a yawn and goes back to bed. No idea of the time, but it doesn't matter. Maybe later, she'll finish counting the steps.

Memory Walk

I wander downhill and join the off-road footpath. Tall conifers line the way, making it dark and damp, although the afternoon is bright and crisp. On the left, an old Norman church built of grey stone, blackened and dark green in places due to centuries of weathering, reclines on a grass bank. Lichened gravestones protrude from the ground at all angles, as if they lacked a sense of symmetry in those days. I remember tracing the touching epitaphs, oblivious to those beneath. Misshapen gargoyles gurn from a stumpy square bell tower, with a clock face the colour of lapis lazuli. A forlorn refrain, like a death knell, chimes as I walk by, reminding the journey is relatively brief, and all things shall pass.

Heavy iron gates lead to an enormous enclosure where a colossal concrete cross dominates on the opposite side. Every November, a sea of blood-red poppies floods the arena, and on that memorable Sunday, locals gather to show respect for those who lost their lives. Aged horse-chestnuts flank the verges, branches bowed as if burdened with unbearable sorrow, leaves falling like silent tears, witnesses to the internment of many loved ones. After school, I came here with friends and threw sticks till the trees rained green, spiked orbs. We cracked them open, hung the shiny brown nuts on strings and smashed them to smithereens.

I cross a narrow metal footbridge over a fast-running brook, tentative footsteps reverberating enough to wake the dead. Three schoolboys ambushed a girl and threw her in. Slim chance of drowning in the two-inch depth, but the experience traumatised her, nevertheless. The brook meanders around a steep hill and disappears beneath a gap in the undergrowth, revealing an entrance and a dirt track leading to the top. A crooked sign poking out the brambles warns: PRIVATE PROPERTY KEEP OUT, which adds to the aura of mystery and compels me to look closer. Craning my neck this way and that, I glimpse a grey stone wall with a castellated roofline, winking through the trees. Why would anyone build a castle here? Nothing of significance, only heathland and rock.

Small in stature but perfectly proportioned, Robert Petit fought bravely in battle for William, Duke of Normandy, and was rewarded with a knighthood and four hectares of land in Witewic, a tiny village in Leicestershire. Known as 'the white farm' due to the chalky soil, the land was useless for growing crops, but the local peasants relied on it for grazing their cattle and sheep.

On Petit's arrival, Hugh de Grandsmil, the newly appointed Sheriff of the Manor, commissioned him to build a motte and bailey castle in all haste.

'Build it on the highest hill', he ordered. 'The land is ours now, and the villagers must answer to me.'

Petit oversaw the construction of the castle, utilising abundant raw materials at hand: timber from the forest for a fortified keep; stone quarried from the rocky outcrops for a courtyard and a high wall; and a natural shallow stream at the base of the hill, he had widened into a moat. Within a month, the castle was complete: an impressive fortification and a magnificent show of wealth and rank from the Norman conquerors.

The Sheriff departed to attend business elsewhere, and Petit took up residence in the tower. For days, he surveyed the surrounding countryside and planned to build a cottage on his plot of land; perhaps rear cows and pigs of his own—perfect for entertaining fellow knights and nobility.

Every morning, a young peasant woman washed in the stream below. Kneeling on the grassy edge she brushed her long fair hair and rinsed her pale complexion in the cool water. Accustomed to going where she pleased without hindrance or prying eyes, she wore her undergarments: a simple linen tunic with a drawstring neck. A beaded bronze necklace, gifted by her father during recent Beltane celebrations, hung around her neck. A proud man, her father descended from a great warrior tribe. At first, he led a band of indigenous folk and rebelled against the invading foreigners: burnt their huts and slew their horses. But beaten into submission, he now accepted his new masters and paid them taxes for the privilege of living and working on the land he once ruled. Life went on. Although, simmering with resentment, he harboured hopes of violent revenge.

Petit spotted the young peasant woman from the tower. From a distance, she made a pleasing shape, and intrigued, he saddled his mare and rode out for a closer look.

Startled by his sudden appearance through the brambles, she gathered her hem, ready to take flight. But Petit raised his right palm, showing he meant no harm.

'Good day, my pretty maid,' he said, smiling.

The young woman's cheeks coloured at the sight of the small handsome knight on his splendid horse, and she looked at the ground.

Captivated, Petit decided there and then, he would marry her, settle down and start a family. Indeed, the Sheriff encouraged such alliances with the indigenous folk.

My dad stood five-foot-six in his winklepickers, relatively small. His brother, Samuel, was a terrier type five-foot-four, but his stoop and the chip he carried made him look much smaller. My father's father was also small, but I only ever saw him flat on his back. He spent his final days bedridden downstairs in the front room of his council house, riddled with cancer, an unsettling gurgle emanating from deep within his chest.

'It's the death rattle,' Mum said. 'It means he hasn't got long left.'

She was right.

After the funeral, a discussion on heredity ensued.

'The first Pettys came over from Spain, as slaves.' My dad was adamant. Admittedly, the name 'Petty' does have a Mediterranean ring. The romantic overtones appeal to some family members; they use it as an excuse for flaring tempers and other unaccountable fits of passion, such as the infidelity gene, apparent in the male line. As marital indiscretions come to light, the Petty women shake their heads and titter, 'It's that Mediterranean temperament.'

But I was despondent. *This is my inheritance.* I glared into Dad's small face, challenging his supposition.

'But how do you know? *How do you know?*'

Fact is, he didn't. It was all hearsay and conjecture, and I comforted myself, knowing there was no evidence to support his claim that my descendants were slaves. No evidence.

The footpath merges back onto the main road. I walk past a white stone cottage, squatting on the corner. A long rectangular window runs the length of the cottage wall, and a tightly knit twelve-foot-high privet hedge envelopes a tiny garden. My brand-new Clarkes shoe once went flying over that hedge, when me and Carole-Anne Baker practised Bruce Lee kicks on our way home from school— Kung Fu, as seen in the films *Enter the Dragon* and *The Way of the Dragon*, was all the rage, as were black faux silk kimonos with gold dragons printed on the back, which I sorely wanted. I limped a mile home in one shoe, and Mum, generally mild-tempered, was distraught because the shoes cost half her housekeeping money. So, we immediately returned to the cottage to retrieve the wayward treasure.

We didn't know who lived there, but we'd heard rumours: Veronica, a spinster in her sixties—nutty as a fruitcake, or so they said—lived there. She roamed the streets all day, boasting of her higher intellect, and claimed she never married because all men are stupid.

'She's just lonely,' Mum said.

The thick oak front door creaked open, and a black cat darted out. Veronica's grey eyes, nervous and suspicious, peered through the gap.

Curious, I glanced past her into the dim room beyond. It was simply furnished with an armchair and a table, no space for much else. A shaft of light through the long window illuminated books piled high on the table.

'Can I have my shoe back, please?' I said, addressing the issue at hand. 'It flew over because of my Bruce Lee kick.'

Veronica glared like *I* was crazy, not understanding the reference.

'They're brand new,' Mum said, as if that explained everything. 'Sorry we disturbed you.'

Veronica looked towards the garden, where the shoe nestled in a rose bush. She waved her hand in affirmation and, sighing at our idiocy, shut the door.

The elongated window shed light on Freda Agnes, as she toiled over her knitting frame. Cramped in a living space barely big enough to hold a bed and a table, she rested a moment to rub her sore eyes and massage her aching back. She opened the thick oak door and gulped air to freshen-up and to stop the hunger pangs breaking her concentration. Later that night, in a shadowy corner of The Three Crowns, fuelled by anger and despair, she urged the other framework knitters to take a stand against the master hosier.

'Evil money-grabbing bastard.' Emaciated and pale, she banged her empty tankard on the table. 'Starving us out of house and home. I can't afford bread, never mind pay the bloody rent, and he's raised the payments on my knitting frame again.'

Old Tom nudged his flat cap further up his balding scalp, revealing bloodshot eyes beneath sagging eyelids. 'Pilfering the poor man's pocket,' he rattled. 'And where's that bit of land the Charity Commission promised, so we can grow our own food?'

'Bloody landowners are busy selling the stone out of it.' Freda Agnes shook her head. 'In any case, when do we have time to cultivate an allotment, tied to that frame fifteen hours a day?'

'Them factories will be the death of us.' Old Tom jabbed the air with his walking stick. 'I'd join Captain Ned Ludd's gang, if I were younger.'

Last month, the knitters refused to work in protest of decreasing wages and high rent, but starving, they soon returned. To make up time, the hosier raised the price of yarn and reduced his payment for completed items.

'2s 6d. I can't pay you anymore', the hosier said. 'Folks can get cheaper now, elsewhere.'

'Ours are better, though!' Freda Agnes made a final desperate plea for the quality of their hand-crafted products. 'That hose they make in factories—sock heels cut with scissors, stretched out and sewn on—falls to bits in no time.' She held out a stocking she had knitted herself. 'Look, see how many stitches and feel the thickness.'

But the master hosier wasn't interested. Profit is what interested him.

Thin as lathes, weak and exhausted, Freda Agnes and Old Tom packed their meagre belongings in a sack and headed for the castellated roofline winking through the trees. Once a fortification for wealthy conquerors, now a hostel for the poor and disenfranchised, the alms-house on the hill was their last beacon of hope.

I reach the end of our street. A man trips out of The Three Crowns, gripping *The Sun* newspaper, opened at the horse racing schedule. Looking over his shoulder down a magnolia passageway, I search for the off-licence window, and recall reaching-up and tapping on the frosted glass, till the lower section raised. The barman couldn't care less if I asked for a bottle of Bells and a packet of Woodbines, but I generally only wanted ten Embassy No 6 and a bar of Cadbury's Fruit and Nut. Mum had scribbled a note, saying the fags were for her and signed it, because only sixteen-year-olds and above could buy cigarettes legally. But the barman didn't read it and handed the goods over with yellow-nicotine-stained-fingers, no questions asked.

Across the road, rhythmic clickety-clicking spills out of arched leaded windows of a red-bricked factory. Inside, electric looms spew various items of hosiery: socks, tights, and stockings, while faceless workers pack them into enormous cardboard boxes. My grandma was manageress here. She wore five-inch platform wedges, despite having water on the knee, corns, and a bunion on her left big toe, which she eventually had surgically corrected. Once a fortnight, the hairdresser dyed her hair jet black, and if it were not for her many lines and wrinkles, which she tried to keep at bay with a plethora of lotions, you might presume she was ten years younger than her actual age. She earned good money, more than Grandad at the pit. Grandad worked as a Bevan boy during the war. When Thatcher closed the mines, he took early retirement with a £10,000 pay-off. The National Coal Board engraved a Davy lamp for him, marking fifty years' service. I keep the lamp on my windowsill. Where we come from matters.

Mum worked at the factory, for a while. She had wanted an office job: learn to type and do the books but failed the eleven plus. She became a checker, instead: rolling stockings over a pole, checking if they had ladders or holes. Eight hours a day. Five days a week. Saturday nights, she went dancing in town. One cold night, late October, it was raining hard and, worried in case she arrived home late because there would be hell to pay, she took a shortcut through Churchyard. At the bottom of Castle Hill, a small man materialised out of the brambles and walked her home. Married at seventeen, she left work to be a mother and full-time housewife.

At last, home. One in a row of terraces of the same ilk: red-bricked. like the factory, with two large square windows facing front: one up, one down. A waist-height wall, rendered in bubbly white cement encloses a twelve-by-six-foot garden, paved with slabs because Dad wasn't one for gardening. The dark-blue metal gate hanging open because the hinges rusted over, making it look like we had a continual flux of visitors who inconsiderately neglected to close it behind them. A square pane of opaque glass in the front door is cracked where Mum missed her aim.

I fumble in the dwindling light and turn the key. The past gets buried, forgotten. I see it all. A re-vision. We all become stories in the end.

About the Author

Sue lives in Leicestershire, UK. She holds a PhD focussed on working-class women's writing and an MPhil specialising in working-class women's autobiography. Her interests include reading radical texts and walking through the local countryside, exploring its rich social history. She is currently working on her nonfiction book, *Working-Class Women Writing Class*.